If Kane didn't get his job back, he was finished . . .

Every gunslinger from Red River to Rio Grande would know that Morgan Kane, *ex-marshal*, was fair game. The idea of gaining instant reputation of revenging past fights; of . . . hell, of anything that struck their fancy, would have them hunting him. Without a star, Kane would be hunted mercilessly. Sooner or later, it'd mean his execution . . . and it'd been for this reason he'd returned to Shane after six months absence. Kane and his star were inseparable, having grown together through the bonding forge of blood and death, and it wasn't fear which made him turn back to it now . . .

Also by Louis Masterson

WITHOUT MERCY
THE CLAW OF THE DRAGON
THE STAR AND THE GUN
BACKED BY THE LAW
A RANGER'S HONOUR
MARSHAL AND MURDERER
PISTOLERO
THE MONSTER FROM YUMA
THE DEVIL'S MARSHAL
GUNMAN'S INHERITANCE
REVENGE
STORM OVER SONORA
THE LAW OF THE JUNGLE
NO TEARS FOR MORGAN KANE
BETWEEN LIFE AND DEATH
RETURN TO ACTION
RIO GRANDE
BRAVADO
THE GALLOWS EXPRESS
RANSOM
KILLING FOR THE LAW
THE BUTCHER FROM GUERRERO
DUEL IN TOMBSTONE
TO THE DEATH, SENOR KANE!
HELL BELOW ZERO
THE DAY OF DEATH
COYOTEROS!
BLOODY EARTH
NEW ORLEANS GAMBLE
APACHE BREAKOUT
BLOOD AND GOLD
SOUTHERN SHOWDOWN
BELL OF DEATH

and published by Corgi Books

Louis Masterson

The Demon From Nicaragua

CORGI BOOKS
A DIVISION OF TRANSWORLD PUBLISHERS LTD

THE DEMON FROM NICARAGUA
A CORGI BOOK 0 552 10331 4

First publication in Great Britain

PRINTING HISTORY
Corgi edition published 1976

Corgi Books are published by Transworld Publishers Ltd.,
Century House, 61–63 Uxbridge Road,
Ealing, London W.5.
Made and printed in Great Britain by
Hunt Barnard Printing Ltd, Aylesbury, Bucks.

The Demon From Nicaragua

THE DEMON FROM NICARAGUA with Morgan Kane

Morgan Kane's ears were ringing as he lowered the heavy .44 Colt double-action revolver. A small cloud of dust drifted around the targets at which he'd been shooting, but Kane hardly waited for it to dissipate before reloading and firing again. He'd taken only a single sharp glance at the target, his expression never changing to indicate either pleasure or disapproval at his score of four bulls and two inners, so intense was his concentration on the job—his job of shooting—first, accurate, and for keeps. His life depended on it.

He'd been practising for two solid hours now, and he could feel it in his arms, shoulders, and legs. He shot in order to become totally familiar with this particular pistol, recently acquired and different from his previous single-action Colt; with its brand-new "Baugham Quick-Draw" foresight, it was the invention of a Chicago policeman to stop the front sight from snagging in one's holster or clothes. The new sight confirmed what Kane and so many other gunman did to pistols—file down the ungainly stub sight and learn to shoot accurately by practice and intuition.

There were four other officers on the practice range with Kane. They were also from the garrison in Fort Leavenworth, Kansas, and made a sort of unofficial gun-club. They pretended not to notice how strangely Kane was acting around the fort; how nervous and irritable he was toward everybody. It was as if he were being pulled tighter and tighter by an invisible rope—a rope that was also helping to hang him internally—and a rope that was about gnawed through and would break soon, leaving him mentally dangling. The four shot their pistols and discussed scores with the same indifferent, calm tones they always did.

Yet when Kane wasn't around, the four as well as the other men talked about their old friend and compatriot, who was now like a stranger among them. It was as if his leaving months before, after throwing down his marshal's badge, had been the death of the Kane they'd known and worked with. When he'd returned a few weeks ago and asked for his job back, it was *not* as if he'd returned from some grave. This Kane was different: harsher, more stubborn and brutal than ever before. The quasi leave-of-absence his commanding officer, Bill Shane, had given him then hadn't softened Kane or returned the old qualities one bit. His reinstatement papers had been processed in Washington and Kane had come back from a trip to California, but it was the *new* Kane which joined them on the practice range and ate with them in the mess hall. It was a Kane which puzzled and perplexed the men who'd grown up with the old Kane, and naturally they talked.

Kane knew they talked about him behind his back, and tried to shrug it off. It rankled him, like an itch he couldn't quite reach, but it didn't pester him that much. Besides, he couldn't really blame his comrades. He wasn't quite sure what was happening inside him, either, only that it was and that he'd changed. Not necessarily for the better. Still, he went through the old routines and familiar motions of before. When he'd returned from California a week ago, he'd checked in with Shane first thing, as a matter of duty and habit and interest to see if his reinstatement papers had been processed. He'd given Shane a rundown on his activities, detailing his experiences while on what was supposed to be a relaxation and recreation trip. Some vacation! He'd recounted the strange adventure he'd had with Lord Raleigh and his sister Eileen, who with another couple, Anthony Garfield and his cousin Fawn Chapman, had been crossing the high Sierras in search of the fabled Zuni Indian treasure of Cibola. Instead of wealth, they'd found escaped convicts from the Arizona Territorial Prison—and as for Garfield and Fawn, they'd found death. The "Golden Man" bell and the seven towns which legend had painted with treasure were left buried under the sands and mesas. Kane had literally stumbled into them, having fallen through a weak crust of earth into a hollowed-out grotto filled with the skeletons of human sacrifices. It was as cursed a place as it was rich, and Kane wasn't interested in disturbing the centuries of legend for rakehell plunderers. He'd left the Raleighs in Yuma after they too decided to forget whatever they might have learned about the site, and he'd returned to Fort Leavenworth and Kansas City.

Shane, hearing this story, sighed a weary sigh. He'd ordered Kane to stay out of mischief, but he might as well have been talking to his chair. Trouble dogged Kane. Things happened when Kane was around the way they never happend to his other marshals. Kane was a pain in the ass—but he was also a valuable man because of his trouble-prone quality, and because he'd learned how to keep himself alive throughout it all. Shane told Kane to wait around the garrison awhile; some of the papers hadn't come through yet and his next assignment depended on them.

Wait! Kane hated to wait! He was tempted to spend the waiting dead drunk, but knew that what chance he had for reinstatement would be shot to hell if he did go on a bender that way. So he spent his hours on the practice range, honing his craft and bleeding some of his discontentment. And waiting . . .

"Kane!"

Morgan Kane swivelled around, lowering his smoking revolver. He saw Shane's adjutant trotting over the crest of the nearest rise, hair streaming in the bluff, squirrelling breeze.

"Mr. Kane, you're wanted. On the double!"

"Thanks." At last! Kane finished his last round, ejected the spent cartridges, and carefully cleaned his pistol. The adjutant fretted and nervously twitched from the delay, and Kane kept him waiting on purpose. He'd been waiting for days, for Christ's sake—let this pipsqueak who wants him to run "on the double" wait a bit himself! Then slowly, Kane began sauntering up the rise to where the main trail to the fort intersected.

A short while later, he entered Shane's spartan office. Shane looked pleased to see him, which immediately put Kane on guard.

"Sir," Kane said casually, sinking into the nearest chair.

Shane glanced at the gunbelt. "Been keeping busy?"

"So-so."

Shane nodded, still smiling. Kane began fidgeting

like the adjutant had done. Shane said after a pause: "Got the final word from Washington, Morgan . . ."

"Yeah?"

"Yeah." Shane shuffled some papers around as if in concentration. Kane tried to keep perfectly still, unruffled, though internally excitement was making him quiver. He hoped his face wouldn't betray how anxious he felt, because then Shane would rub it in even more than he was already, good news or bad. *Final word* . . . How final that in itself sounded! If Washington denied his reinstatement now, it would mean newspaper headlines throughout the territory. Every gun-slinger from Red river to Rio Grande would know that Morgan Kane, *ex-marshal*, was fair game. The idea of gaining instant reputation; of revenging past fights; of . . . hell, of anything that struck their fancy, would have them hunting him. Without a star, Kane would be hounded mercilessly. Sooner or later, it'd mean his execution—and it'd been for this reason he'd returned to Shane after six months absence. Kane and his star were inseparable, having grown together through the bonding forge of blood and death, and it wasn't fear which made him turn back to it now. It was prudence. The acknowledgement that he could exist for awhile without the badge, but that he couldn't be *alive*.

Not that those pencil-pushing desk sergeants in Washington understood such things. No, they only went by records and files and memorandums and rule books, their opinions as dog-earred as their ledgers, and Kane didn't have any hopes toward swaying their verdict. Still, Shane had recommended reinstatement, and that'd carry weight—maybe. And now Shane was savouring this last indulgence, this little bit of victory for the pride he'd lost when Kane had thrown his badge down and walked out a half a year ago.

"Yep," Shane repeated. "The word came through, the final word about your future, Morgan. You're back on."

Kane closed his eyes, knowing he was sighing even though he didn't want to show the slightest emotion now.

"But not without conditions," Shane continued. "A period of probation, Morgan. Six months—which seems a fitting time, considering how long you decided to play the horse away from here—six months and if you screw up once, just once, you're out for good."

Kane nodded—what was there for him to say?

Shane made a noncommittal grunt and picked up one of the papers in front of him. "The Department of State," he read out loud, tapping the embossed seal heading the letter.

"You mean *they* okayed me? But I thought—"

"No, no of course not, Morgan. But your final approval didn't clear till they came up with this and passed it on to the Justice Department. Case of one hand washing the other, if you see what I mean."

Kane wasn't sure he did, but kept silent, positive there was more to come. And undoubtedly unpleasant, if it was filtering down from such heights as the State Department. Obviously he'd been rehired on the basis of one assignment—one which he could figure automatically as being dangerous and probably lethal. They wouldn't have handed it to him otherwise. And if he did manage to return breathing, he could be blackballed for bad behaviour.

A sour taste grew in Kane's mouth, the bitter gall of irony, as he listened to Shane explain about the letter.

"They want you to take a trip, Morgan. To Panama."

"Panama? You mean . . . in Central America?"

"Uh-huh. The department in the country of Colombia that makes up the little neck between the Atlantic and Pacific oceans."

Kane, having jerked upright from the news, settled in the chair again, trying to recall what he knew about the insignificant stretch of territory. Practically nothing. But then he didn't know much about Colombia or the other countries along that belt like Guatemala, Honduras, Nicaragua and Costa Rica. Spanish possessions for the most part, some having won independence, prone to a revolution a week and a chronic thorn in the side of Britain and the United States. What the hell could anyone want him down there for?

"It's over a canal," Shane said, as if reading Kane's thoughts. "I'm sure you've read about speculations on building a canal from one ocean to the other. The Big Ditch, the papers call it."

"Yeah . . . Yeah, now that you mention it, I have. But the talk's been going on a long time and nothin's been done about it."

"Since the fifteen hundreds, there's been talk. It'd cut thousands of miles off the voyage around the Cape. It'd slice travel time in half 'tween New York and San Francisco, it's estimated. I mean, after the gold rush in California and the wagon trains out there, it's come down to the fact that what the Europeans thoughts would be nice, we damn well need." Shane opened a lower drawer of his desk, took out a rolled-up map, and spread it across his desk. "Here, hold down a corner and look at this."

Kane rose, hunching over the map and following Shane's finger as it traced a course across the outline of Central America.

"There's two main choices for the canal location," Shane said. "One is between Colon and Panama City—the Panama Canal. The other is through Nicaragua, using this big lake here, Lago de Nicaragua and its river, Rio San Juan. The San Juan flows eastward from the lake to the Caribbean, and the U.S. Army Corps of Engineers figure it's possible to dig a canal from the Pacific to the lake and then use the river the rest of the way."

"But the Panama route is a lot shorter."

"Geographically it is, but not politically. Panama wants to be independent of Colombia, and naturally Colombia wants to hold onto it, so there've been lots of riots and killings and the rest of that kind of thing. Still, canal rights have been negotiated. The French in '78 and then again in '79 have put a lot of capital into it and after a bitch of a fight, the French government approved a guarantee of the loans. But last news on the project is that disease, corruption and just plain incompetence has pretty much put a halt to the venture. Bankruptcy is expected."

"What about us? You said we're the ones who need such a ditch."

"I'm coming to us, Morgan. Washington figures that with Ferdinand de Lessep's French 'Transoceanic International Civil Channel Corporation' in Panama, we'd better get cracking in Nicaragua."

"But why? Wouldn't the French let us use their canal too?"

"Sure, but the boys at State figure maybe times will change and we'd best have the licence and control than some foreign power. So four years ago we made a pact with Nicaragua—the Frelinghuyser-Zarala Agreement—that also included Costa Rica, since the San Juan River is on its border, and we'd probably want to widen it while we're at it. Now, the Senate turned it down, but a bunch of businessmen have gone through with it on a private basis. They've formed the Nicaragua Canal Company, been raising money, and have actually started digging."

"And?"

"And they've practically ground to a halt."

"Like the French in Panama, eh?"

"Worse. To the list of graft and disease and stupidity, you can add outright sabotage. The State Department wants to know why. Who's behind the mess down there. Who's scaring the workers away and who's poisoning the food and . . . hell, you know what I mean."

"Sure, I guess I do. But you said this was a private deal."

"I said, Morgan, that the Senate refused to pass the funds, but that the administration backed the bill. The administration is as eager as any of the investors to get that canal through, so they've authorized you to go down there and tell them what's what."

"Authorized me to do it—unofficially, is that it?"

"Well, you're not going in there like the Marines, no. The consuls in Panama City, Colon, and Puerto Limon will give you what help they can, but by and large, you'll be in Nicaragua on your own."

Shane lapsed silent. Kane said after a moment: "That's it?"

"Ain't it enough, Morgan?"

Kane looked out the window behind Shane, speaking slowly and evenly. "I've got a feeling that for you and Washington, it's never going to be enough. I take this on, or I take on nothing. No backing, and if I make a mis-step, I'm dead or out of the force." He sighed, shaking his head, then slapped dust from his trouser leg. "Alright, how do I get there and when do I leave?"

"Boat from New Orleans on Friday," Shane answered briskly, ignoring Kane's remarks. "The consul in Colon will be expecting you."

"I hope it was better than the last garbage scow I was on."

"The boat? Oh it's a good one. The new *Caribbean Queen* on the Atlantic and Caribbean Lines. We're handling the train for you too."

"Thanks," Kane said wryly.

"Thank me when you get back. Oh—and get yourself some fancy-dress tropical duds, quinine against the mosquitoes, and a money belt."

"I've got a money belt."

"Then we'll scrape up some dinero for you tomorrow. That's all."

Kane scraped the chair back and stood. He looked at Shane, wanting to say something but unable to think what, and finally he gave up, pivoted on his heel and stalked toward the door. Behind him, he heard Shane cough and call out: "Morgan?"

Kane froze, not turning, his hand on the door knob.

"I, ah . . . Good luck, Morgan."

"Thanks, sir."

Kane went out, closing the door behind him. Walking down the corridor, he frowned, thinking that his assignment and Shane's quick dealing of the information was somehow wrong. How could Shane have managed to make those train and boat reservations so fast? Or had he known all along that he, Kane, would be taken back into the force and be sent by Washington out of the country? Had Shane purposely made him sweat for days out on the practice range, just like he'd made him uncomfortable in his office? Was it an indication of the clout Shane wielded and wanted to prove?

It had to be that!

Kane gritted his teeth, anger seething through him. He'd been used, and was going to be used further, and there wasn't a damn thing he could do about it. Shane had deliberately made him sweat, as a demonstration and a warning.

Kane decided to take the warning seriously.

2

The heavily-muscled, half-naked choco-Indian finished the last dregs of the mug, then went behind the shack to relieve himself. He gazed down as he stood in the shadows, down at the gaping wound in the jungle landscape. In the hazy dusk, he could make out the giant steam-engines, and the light-brown clay from the channel they had been digging. Earlier that day there'd been three hundred and fifty, maybe four hundred men down there with the machines, like ants toiling in gruel. There was some-

2

thing eerie and sinister about the empty, deep canyon now; man-made without *its* men, unnatural in this vast green sea of wildlife.

Turning slightly, the native could see the shining gleam of Lago de Ometepe, its waters as still as the ditch below. The work was parallel to the San Juan River, roughly a hundred yards between the two banks, and was temporarily halted while a large hillock of rock was being dynamited. There were always delays, he thought. He had a feeling that there always would be; that this Americano project would never stab through the low mountains and tropical forests, with its fancy series of locks and sluices. He didn't understand how it could. He was merely a foreman, one of the fifty who oversaw the common labourers, and he wasn't hired to think.

"Georgio," the white engineers would tell him, "Georgio, you go get them bastards off'n their butts and shovelling the dirt. We'll go about telling you where they can put it."

So that's what Georgio did. It was a good job, an honourable one, paying more than he'd ever seen before in his whole life. Georgio had come to get work at the canal project just like hundreds of other natives had from all over Nicaragua—Indians, mulattoes, negroes, mestis—to get paid in silver and lose it quickly in the camp town which travelled just behind the digging. Many who arrived weren't hired, because they were diseased or feeble with sores and wounds, and these were driven away with kicks and cuffs. They trailed behind the camp town, like vultures following their victims; stealing and swindling, maybe even killing if they thought they could make a couple of coins and get away with it.

Georgio held these scavengers in contempt,

just as he did the mestis from the coast and others who weren't pure blood and from the jungle. He even felt contempt for the *Americanos* who were hiring him—they of such pale skin, always getting sick, determined to build this stupid ditch across the land! Eh, but they paid him well. He wouldn't tell them they were crazy until they stopped handing across the money. He wasn't stupid like them!

Only one dark cloud fouled Georgio's horizon. It had come about from an incident ten days before, when he and his *compadre* Juan were stopped by a giant mulatto. The mulatto looked very mean and had a large revolver stuck in his belt to back up his expression. Georgio wasn't exactly afraid of this or any other mulatto, but he figured it'd be wise to show respect for the gun.

"My boss," the mulatto told them, "wants to talk to you."

"Who's your boss?" Juan asked.

"Never you mind. You just move on along with me. *Vanamos!*" The mulatto had pulled the revolver then, and Georgio and Juan decided to go along and speak to the boss. They walked out of the camp for a short way, finally reaching a miserable lean-to tent set way back in the shadows of the jungle. The mulatto told them to take off their hats, and they'd whipped off their low straw sombreros before entering the tent. Inside, in the dismal light of a kerosene lantern, they'd seen two sweating white men sitting at a table. One was drinking from a bottle of rum.

The second asked sharply: "Which of you is Georgio?"

"I," Georgio acknowledged.

"Then the other is Juan," the white said as a matter of fact, and took the bottle from the first man.

After a long sip, he continued: "You're foremen, right?"

Georgio and Juan both nodded. "For the canal company."

"Uh-huh." The white men didn't offer them any rum, and the Indians didn't expect any, either. They stood uncomfortably inside the stifling, stinking tent, not liking the white men and hating the mulatto with his pistol even more. "You get five dollars a month," the second white said, and then to their surprise, he smiled. His mouth was filled with gold teeth, which glittered in the feeble light. "Five dollars, and do y'know, down in Panama, foremen are getting twenty-five a month?"

Georgio and Juan just stood there, not knowing what to say.

"Well, did you know?"

"No, sir," Juan answered at last.

"Didn't think so. The Americanos wouldn't want that kind of information to leak out. If it did, why . . . Why you'd want the same amount, wouldn't you?"

"We're satisfied," Juan said, shrugging.

"Five here is more'n twenty-five up there," Georgio added. "And it is only on what we hear, not what we see."

"You're hearing it from me," the man snarled. "From *me*! Matt, you show these stupid buggers, since they want to see things."

The mulatto swept each of the Indians into the crooks of his arms, choking them until they saw stars, their legs dangling off the ground. As big and muscular as they were, they were no match for this monster of a man. He pressed and pressed, making low grunting noises in the back of his throat, while they struggled futilely.

"Alright, Matt, let them go."

The mulatto released them. Georgio and Juan sprawled onto the dirt floor of the tent, rubbing their necks and sucking in air.

The white leaned forward to stare down at them. "Twenty-five bucks a month in Panama. That's for you two and any other foremen who want to work there. We'll be back in a week for your answer, and it'd better be yes. *Comprendo?*"

"Si . . . Si . . ."

"Bueno. Now get the hell outta my sight . . ."

Ten days since then, and still no sign of the white men's return. But plenty of other foremen and workmen had heard about their offer of fabulous money further south in Panama, rumours and stories flooded the camp and worksite, becoming enflamed from *pinga*—cheap sugar-cane alcohol everybody drank in the evenings. Resentment festered, grumblings turning into outright defiance. *Americanos* were spat upon, tools were stolen, machines were damaged. Spades, pick-axes, even wheelbarrows disappeared . . . only to reappear after trips to clandestine blacksmithies, but now fashioned into crude machetes and knives. The white men had done more than offer more money—they'd sown discontent that was threatening to become a revolt.

Georgio could smell death in the air. It had a tangy odour to it that chilled his bones and made him think of blood. He walked downcast back into his tiny shack, sitting down again and reaching for the pinga and his mug. It helped him to forget about the men and the week which had stretched into ten days. . . .

Less than an hour later, the white men came to him. They didn't bother knocking; the mulatto kicked the door in. Georgio could see the two men behind the mulatto, partially hidden in the thick foliage of the surrounding trees so that they were deeply shadowed figures without distinct expressions. The mulatto said:

"Turn up the light."

"What do you want?" Georgio asked, already knowing the answer. He reached out as if to raise the light in his lantern, then swivelled to snatch up a machete beside the leg of the table. The mulatto was faster. He struck at the table, upending it against Georgio and sending him sprawling, then casually reached down to pick up the machete.

"Turn up the light," the mulatto repeated, and this time Georgio obeyed. From the lantern suspended by a wire from the ceiling, a yellow light spread outward to detail the mulatto's gnarled features, and then those of the white men as they stepped inside the shack. The one who'd done all the talking last time had the face of a toad—broad and flat, covered with mottled flesh. The other had a pinched face, offset by a curved beak of a nose. Both wore filthy white linen shirts and lightweight trousers, plus Sam Browne belts slung around their shoulders and weighted down with cartridges, holsters, and heavy pistols.

"What do we want!" the leader sneered. "Ain't that a hot one, as if you've forgotten, Georgio. Well, I want to know if you accept our offer or not."

"What offer?" Georgio could feel his parched lips, and licked them with a dry tongue. Sometimes if he acted really stupid, white men believed it and left him alone. "What offer, señor?"

"Twenty-five a month in Panama as a foreman, you idiot."

"Oh no, señor, I couldn't take that."

"Why not?"

"It's too far away. It'd take much money to get there."

"Money, money, always more money. You'll walk, comprendo?"

"But I like it here, señor, I am sorry."

"So am I, Georgio. And since you like it here so much, why, we'll arrange it so you can be sure and stay. Matt!"

The mulatto jumped into action before Georgio had time to react. The mulatto knocked him down, stunned him, then tied his arms behind his back with a strip of rawhide. He hoisted Georgio around on the filthy dirt, snaking one sandal off and stuffing it in Georgio's open mouth so he couldn't scream. Another leather thong held it tightly in place; Georgio had trouble even to suck in air, and the taste of the sandal was foul. He writhed in anger and humiliation, and yes, he had to admit, in fear.

"On the cot with him, Matt," the white man ordered.

Georgio was tossed on his cot as if he were a child. He watched with ever bulging eyes as the mulatto approached with Georgio's own machete. "No, no," he tried to cry out, but nothing but muffled groans escaped from around the sandal. The mulatto smiled maliciously, bringing the machete down against Georgio's leg. Georgio tried to squirm free, but the mulatto held him like a hind quarter of beef, scalping the hairs off the back of Georgio's right leg, down from the knee along the calf to his heel. The mulatto paused at the heel—then made a quick, deft slice across Georgio's Achilles tendon. The shock didn't register for a moment, and then it set in, along with the pain.

Georgio arched off the cot, staring down at his oddly angled, now useless foot. He'd never walk right again! Hardly any blood seeped from the wound, and in a way, that made his injury all the worse. He stared at himself, acute agony snapping up through his leg, mixing with the horror of being a cripple forever—until he couldn't stand it any longer. He flopped back on the cot, fainting away.

The three men left his shack without another word. . . .

That same night, another "accident" took place in the camp. The storage shed along the northern edge of the canal caught fire, the dry wood and canvas going up in a towering sheet of flame, igniting paraffin and lubricating oil and other combustibles stored nearby. From the huts and tents of the workers, the site looked as if a volcano had suddenly erupted on its spot. Its red glare could be seen all the way to the village of La Cruz, on the shore of Lago de Nicaragua. . . .

As the fire raged out of control, the two white men lounged in a small cafe at the far end of the tent town. The toadish-looking man glanced at his watch, nodding with pleasure.

"On the dot," he said to the other man. "This and Georgio's accident should be quite effective, I think. Streicher, you owe me ten bucks."

Franz Streicher picked up a thin wallet and took out a banknote. "Alright, you won this bet. But let's get the hell out of here."

"No hurry, no wurry. Matt placed those explosives good and proper. It's obvious that fire won't be controlled tonight."

"I don't want to take chances, Kanter."

"Exactly. You want to chance the jungle at night? Tomorrow we'll head for the coast when there's more light to go by than just from the fire."

Matt didn't say anything throughout their conversation, contentedly listening to the whites and dreamily pleased with having done a good job at setting the fire. The mulatto liked setting fires—yes, and cutting tendons, too. Four he'd cut tonight, and it gave him a sense of artistic ability doing it, in contrast to the usual beatings and kickings he did. Kanter was a smart man, thinking of the tendons. Clever, and a good boss. . . .

Streicher was asking: "Where'll we go next?"

"Tonight? To a woman, Franz, to a woman of course."

"I mean when we get to the coast tomorrow."

"South, I figure, maybe down to Colon. I want to get this yellow fever and malaria belt behind me while I'm still well."

"I know what you mean," Streicher agreed, nodding.

Kanter touched the mulatto on his sleeve. "Matt, why don't you meet us tomorrow, eh?"

"Yeah." The mulatto rose, knowing that he was being asked to leave. That was all right; Kanter's talk of a woman had aroused him, and like always, Kanter was right. A woman would feel fine about now, after a good job. He left the cafe and walked down the shanty-town's main street—which was also its only street, a muddy, rutted track between the tents and crude shacks. He walked until he came to a low, round tent with some young Indian girls lazing around its open flap, chattering with idle gossip. When they saw him approach, they all grinned encouragingly at him, a few making ribald comments. He chose the most brazen of them. She was perhaps thirteen, flatnosed with round, button eyes and gourd-like breasts despite her youth. She sashayed up to him and grabbed the crotch of his pants in one hand.

Matt grinned broadly, letting her lead him into the tent.

Later, while the mulatto was still occupied in the crib, Kanter and Streicher left the cafe and sauntered the other direction. It didn't make much difference which way one went; eventually they came to the outskirts of the town and the same sort of bawdy display of goods and services. But uptown had a bit more class, Kanter figured, by offering a bed and a shack along with the girl.

They stopped in front of the stoop of one shanty, looking at a slim girl who stood naked except for a thin grass skirt. Her mother sprawled in the doorway, wheezing through layers of fat while guaranteeing her daughter was a virgin. Streicher glanced at the girl, not particularly interested, but Kanter was watching every motion the girl made, spittle forming at the sides of his mouth.

"Two bucks," Kanter said to the woman. "Not a penny more."

"Señor! My own flesh and blood, a virgin!"

"She's about as much a virgin as you are."

The woman laughed. "I am too, señor. Who'd want me, eh?"

"How old is she?"

"Twelve last week, I swear by the saints."

"Two bucks."

"You're ruining me!"

"At least I ain't ruining your daughter."

The mother rolled her eyes in desperation. "Ah, if it weren't for the fire tonight and nobody here to enjoy her properly. . . ."

"Save the sobs for another sucker. Two bucks or nothing."

"*Si, si,* then two dollar it is. In advance."

Kanter paid. He and the girl, along with Streicher, went into the fetid square shack, while the mother shut the door and kept watch on the stoop for other customers. Kanter grinned at the girl, running one hand along her developing breasts and pinching her nipples. She didn't react, not even wincing, but just stared at him the way a cow might, with placid eyes.

"What's your name, girl?"

"Chilita, señor."

"You dance, Chilita?"

"*Si.* I show?"

"Yeah." Kanter nudged Streicher, who was inspecting his short-barrelled pocket revolver. "Hey, put that banker's special away and join in, Franz."

"This moist air makes everything rust," Streicher replied.

"Except the girls," Kanter chuckled. "They grow more precocious. Look at 'er, willya? Another coupla years as a twelve-year-old virgin, and she'll be overripe as her mama."

Chilita was dancing, blocking out the crude conversation between the two men. It was a dance not of native Indian origin, but one which white men had taught her, the same way they'd taught her how to make love to them. Streicher watched along with Kanter, but not with pleasure. He felt moody, irritable, wanting to be away from this pretty child and this dank hovel. He wished he were with some experienced, buxom wench in a luxurious hotel in

Colon or Panama City. That's what made all this damn work worth while, he thought; the rich life he could afford along with the shipowners and engineers that followed in the wake of the canal project.

Yeah. . . . In a few days he'd be respectable and clean again, having a perfect dinner on a balcony overlooking the harbour of Colon. Polynesian servants would be gliding around, and the orchestra would be playing a fascinating rhythm across the cedarwood floor. The rich, the beautiful, the adventurous wives and mistresses would be flocking around to seduce or be seduced. In *style*, not like this! This, he decided as he stared at Chilita's bobbing breasts, was down in the mud along with the rest of the Indians and mulattos and bums who never could make it up in the world. He didn't want any part of it, and spurred by his abhorrence, he abruptly stalked toward the door.

"Hey, Franz where're you heading?"

"Out for fresh air. Besides, you don't need me here now."

The girl had stopped dancing and looked at Streicher with the same bland expression as she'd given Kanter. Nothing seemed to please her, not any longer. She was just meat on the hoof.

Kanter was not quite so pliable. He snarled at Streicher: "Yah, well go screw your gun, then. Jesus, I sometimes think you must, the way that's all that seems to matter to you. Go on, get!"

Streicher walked out, almost tripping on the mother.

She grinned up at him. "No like my daughter?"

Streicher raised the revolver and levelled it at her. Her eyes suddenly widened, and she opened her mouth to scream. He pulled the trigger. It fell with a click, for the pistol was empty. He smiled at the mother, feeling better inside now.

"She ain't a virgin," he told her by way of explanation, and walked back down the street toward the cafe.

3

Morgan Kane made a face at himself, watching his reflected image in a mixture of disgust and grim humour. Damn, he looked like the south end of a horse going north, he did!

And that smirking tailor who'd sold him these dude clothes back in New Orleans had fairly wrung his hands with glee. Kane knew when he'd gone into that fancy shop that he had no business in there. But proper tropic gear was needed for him to meet the consul. So Kane had said "yes" to every damn suggestion the tailor made, not knowing what else to do, and had stumbled back out again under a load of parcels and boxes. For two days at sea, he hadn't gotten up the nerve to unwrap all the kaboodle, stubbornly keeping to his own clothes despite the fact he was booked in First Class. He'd stuck to his cabin as much as he could, sweating and drinking beer, hearing the other passengers parading by in their light clothing. He'd glance despairingly at the unopened boxes, wondering when if ever he'd get the nerve to get all duded up and strut out like he was some kind of rooster in a hen-yard. Then he'd get all queasy and uncomfortable, and open another beer instead. For two days it'd been that way, and his courage had not gotten up to the challenge yet.

It was desperation that drove him to getting dressed instead.

The steward, now rather worried about his strangely shy guest, told him that the Captain was having a dress dinner that evening. If Señor Kane was too ill to attend, a doctor would be summoned, but otherwise, the steward would be glad to lay out Señor Kane's dinner outfit. Kane, stunned and perplexed, didn't want the steward to touch the boxes—but he didn't want any sawbones asking a bunch of fool questions, either. He gave in as gracefully as he could, drinking yet another beer while staring reproachfully at the steward unpacking the boxes.

The steward clucked and murmured appreciative things, inwardly shaking his head at Kane's peculiar habit of keeping such fine apparel in its boxes.

Did Señor Kane wished to be dressed . . . ?

"Out!" Kane ordered gruffly. "I'll do my own damn duding, you little monkey!"

That evening, Kane made his debut. With his sunbronzed, lean figure and lined, angular features to highlight it, the white linen suit blazed with perfection. Underneath was a silk shirt with a genteel pleat running down the front; he'd absolutely refused when the tailor had suggested one with ruffled cuffs. The trousers were cut high and *too* tight: there wasn't anyplace to sling a revolver or cartridge belt, but he told himself one would scarcely be necessary on board the *Caribbean Queen*.

Still itchy and discomfited, he strolled as casually as he could down the ship's deck, fiddling now and then with the brim of his Panama, a wide-brimmed hat which according to the tailor just *had* to be worn, but which to him, was a piece of tomfool trash that wouldn't stay right on his head no matter what. It kept sliding over one brow or the other, occasionally tilting back and letting his hair flop loose across his forehead. It was Fashionable, the tailor had assured him. Well, Kane didn't care how fashionable his outfit was. When he sat down in it, it was literally a pain in his ass! The only consolation was that all the other gentlemen in the first class section were similarly dressed in monkey suits.

Kane stuck to the upper first class part, though frequently he glanced down to the second class. He'd travelled by ship quite often, though this was only his third real voyage of any great distance, and the very first time he was up with the ritzy snobs used to luxury, instead of down with the barnacles and peons. The *Queen* was just under four thousand tons, powered by coal-burning steam engines, and truly the regal queen of the Caribbean run since her inauguration the previous year. The smell of fresh paint still lingered, and the handrails were shiny with lacquer instead of age. There were two yardarms and masts, theoretically there for sails should the engines quit, but Kane had a feeling they wouldn't be a great deal of good. He hoped in case of an emergency, that he'd be proven wrong.

So Kane attended dinner that night, leaving his cabin for the steward to clean up. Besides the mountain of beer bottles, it held little except his old clothes, his revolver, belt, and extra shells; and a case of quinine he'd been talked into at the last minute before leaving New Orleans. Into the salon he strolled, still feeling the idiot, but the headwaiter treated him with great deference, as if he were a visiting duke. He was seated next to the Captain's table, in front of a gleaming table cloth lined with assorted knives, forks and spoons like keys on a piano. Kane had absolutely no idea which end of what to start with when the food arrived, and figured he'd best keep a sharp eye on his table's other diners to see what they did.

The other diners consisted of a fat, florid coal dealer from Chicago by the name of Chelmar; his prissy assistant, Miss Wilkinson; and a melancholy reporter from some New York newspaper who said his name was Irving Randolph. Kane introduced himself in a low, gravelly voice, upset now because there was a reporter at the same table who might recognize who he was, despite his fancy disguise. That'd be all he needed!

Instead, Randolph ordered aperitifs, rambling on: "I trust the chef doesn't burn the filet of flounder tonight. I see it's the first course, and I love fish as a rule."

Kane glanced at the filet when it arrived. It was still alive as far as he was concerned, balefully swimming in a private ocean of salad, cucumber, tomato, and pimento. He poked at it with a dainty fork, seeing that's what the others were doing, wondering if there was such a thing as a plate of beans to be had. From now on he'd insist on riding Second Class!

There was a separate bottle of wine for each course, and it took Kane two hours of anguished torment to get through it all. He felt like that proverbial bull in a china shop, and he could see that he was causing Miss Wilkinson a great deal of amusement. He fumbled and moved his food about in his awkward manner, glancing up to see her laughing eyes studying his ridiculous movements. She was wearing a light blue and white dress buttoned from her toes to her neck, and the spectacles perched on her nose bobbed as she nodded at this or that.

Randolph seemed to become more interested in Kane as the meal progressed. Kane tried to avoid Randolph's increasingly sharp gaze, not wanting to look at the hound-dog expression, the tubby vested belly and glittering gold watch-chain of the reporter. But Miss Wilkinson was directly across from him, catching the stray glances Kane was giving in his attempt to keep away from Randolph, and Chelmar kept trying to strike up a conversation each time Kane strayed toward him.

"Yes," Randolph said slowly, thoughtfully.

"Yes, what?" Miss Wilkinson asked politely.

"Yes, I'm sure now. I'm sure I've seen you someplace before." He was addressing Kane, pointing at him with the prongs of his fork.

"Impossible," Kane muttered. "Have some more wine."

"Don't mind if I do. Mr Kane . . . Kane . . . Morgan Kane?"

"None for me, thank you," Miss Wilkinson said to Kane as he tried pouring wine into her goblet. "I've had quite enough as it is, and I'm sure Mr Chelmar wouldn't want me tipsy."

"Not at all, Miss Wilkinson," Chelmar said. "Perhaps a bit of wine might get you to stop eating hardtack for breakfast."

"I beg your pardon, I eat scones." Miss Wilkinson drew back, adjusting her spectacles to give her employer a cold stare. "Hardtack, indeed. I dare say after fifteen years in the United States, I haven't sunk to the point of *being* a common sailor."

"Hardly, Miss Wilkinson," Chelmar replied, and belched into his napkin. "Well, I'll take some more wine, I believe."

Kane poured dutifully, wishing he'd stayed in his cabin and risked the doctor's visit instead. Randolph was still staring at him, frowning now as if on the verge of the answer.

"Your face," Randolph murmured. "I've seen your face."

"I doubt it," Kane told him evenly, wanting to squash the reporter's nosy intrusion.

"Ah, but I have. I'll remember it, give me time. . . ."

"Where are you heading, Mr Chelmar?" Kane asked hurriedly, changing the subject. "Panama or further on?"

"Panama," Chelmar responded. "I'm going to see how my investment's doing in Nicaragua—it's this canal dig, you know—but I want to see how the French are faring first."

"Terrible," Randolph said then. "One long scandal."

"If the Lord had wanted a sea route through Central America," Miss Wilkinson said primly, "He would have placed one there."

"Yes, yes, m'dear." Chelmar looked at the others. "Miss Wilkinson is a loyal secretary, even when she doesn't believe in the business I transact. And you, Mr Randolph? Are you going to report on the French?"

"On the Americans," Randolph said. "On the few Americans who're living in luxury while the poor starving natives are dying off like flies from disease and neglect. It's a scandal too."

"Why, I understood it was we Americans who're dying from fever and malaria down there."

"More yellow journalism than yellow fever, Mr Chelmar. It makes for good circulation and gets people all excited at home, but the truth is that there're only about fifty of us living down there. Engineers, technicians, navy personnel . . . all living like sultans on corruption and never getting their boots dirty once."

"Whoever is dying, I think it's a shame."

"Yes, Miss Wilkinson, it is a shame. I hope to wake the public up to the fact, but I. . . ." Randolph shook his head, sighing. "I doubt I'll be very successful. Our own negroes die of smallpox and nobody turns a hair. It's only if one of us gets it that somebody notices and thinks something should be done. But I want to get to the bottom of the worst scandal in American history—yes, and in French history as well—and I promise to do so."

Kane, during this conversation, had been pushing his chair slowly back, out of the reporter's line of sight. Now he rose, mumbling an apology, and excused himself. He turned to go, and almost stepped on the foot of a young woman who'd come up behind him. "Oh, I'm sorry," he said, sinking in his chair again.

Kane received a flash of white teeth and a gorgeous smile in acknowledgement. The girl had an oval face, nicely tanned in contrast to the usual ivory complexions of the surrounding ladies, and a lithe figure with small breasts and almost boyish thighs. "My fault entirely," she said to him, then turned to Randolph. "Hello, Irving."

Randolph was standing now, brushing himself off. "Ah, Gwen! Here, let me introduce you. Miss Wilkinson, Mr Chelmar, both of Chicago and coal, and Mr Kane. This is Miss Gwen—"

"Doctor, Irving."

"No! You actually made it all the way through medical school?"

"On my honour. But it's still sort of a secret."

"Well, well, fancy that. *Doctor* Gwen Arling, everybody."

Gwen found a chair from the adjoining table, and drew it up between Randolph and Kane. Kane, no longer so eager to leave, gazed over at her, distrustful of any lady who was so young and lovely and had a doctor's diploma. He wouldn't trust her with a broken finger, he concluded—or himself while she was treating it.

"We were on the subject of the canals," Randolph said to her. "Are you going down there as part of your new career?"

Gwen nodded. "There's a small group of us going down to see what we can learn about this yellow fever and malaria. There's a theory going around that it's transmitted by insects, but it'll take a great deal of research to properly check and diagnose the cause."

"What about the poor souls who have these diseases?" Miss Wilkinson asked, adjusting her spectacles. "More important than insects, wouldn't you say, young lady?"

"Unfortunately, Miss Wilkinson, until we know more, we can't save anybody. All we can do is hand out quinine and hope for the cure eventually." Gwen turned to Randolph. "And you're no doubt on one of your head-hunting expeditions, Irving. Out for blood with your quill pens and black ink."

"Your diagnosis is correct this time." Randolph smiled at her, his heavy face becoming creased with lines. "You're a pestilence and a plague of your own, you know, ever since you grew up next door to me back in Virginia. Always wanting me to write your school reports for you in exchange for darning my socks."

"Well, it worked out fine for both of us, didn't it?"

"Childhood schemes, Gwen, and you haven't grown up yet."

"Interesting," Chelmar cut in, always ready with his own anecdote. "When I was a child, I was digging in tunnels. Now look where I am. It just goes to show you."

Kane wasn't quite sure what it went to show, but wasn't able to ponder on the philosophy as the doctor turned to ask him: "And you, Mr Kane? Is there a connection with your boyhood too?"

"Only that I'm a product of it, Ma'am," he answered, not smiling. He wanted no part of recalling his painful youth.

"Ha! I've got it," Randolph said. "I *have* seen your face!"

"Who, Mr Kane's?"

"Yes, Gwen. A picture snapped by . . . by . . . Fly, Camillus Fly, that's who, out in Arizona somewhere. Mr Kane was drawing his gun right at the camera. A remarkable photo. Won third prize in a contest up in Boston, that's where I saw it."

Kane looked ceilingward, beyond speaking. He felt all eyes drawn to him, and his own blood began to rise in his neck.

Gwen said, "Why, I hardly believe that this gentleman—"

"No, no I'm sure," Randolph interrupted emphatically. "There was a reporter writing up about Mr Kane, too. Not mister—Marshal Kane! That's right, and let me see, the reporter's name was. . . .

A woman, she was . . . Goodman, no, Cullman . . . Coleman, Kate Coleman!"

"My heavens!" Miss Wilkinson exclaimed, "A policeman!"

"I can prove it, too," Randolph continued. "Mr Kane, hold up your hands, will you? Marshal Kane has a bad little finger which sticks out straight unless he keeps it tied down with a leather sleeve. I read about that, I know I did."

But Kane remained motionless, gritting his teeth and refusing to be drawn into this spectacle. Gwen said after a long pause: "I think you're being rather rude, Irving."

"Rude! Why, Marshal Kane in person to interview would be a scoop! Of course I'm rude, and I'll be a darn sight—"

"Please excuse him, Mr Kane," Gwen cut in. "Excuse all of us."

"That's perfectly alright," Kane managed to reply. He stood, forcing himself to smile wanly. "Now, if you'll excuse me. . . ."

"Hold on for just a moment, Mr Kane. Or Marshal Kane, if you prefer." Gwen was staring at him, her lips compressed. "We've been rude, but it wouldn't be fair for me to give you the wrong impression. I too have read about you, and I'm appalled."

"I don't wish to argue, Ma'am. Or discuss myself with you."

"But why are you so appalled, Miss Arling?" Chelmar asked. "I understand he's a law officer. Has he done something wrong?"

Gwen had her hand on Kane's jacket, holding him from leaving. "Mr Chelmar, this man hides behind his badge to kill people. He's a murderer, a cold-blooded murderer, using the law as his protection."

"Oh boy," Randolph laughed. "There it goes, folks! If I was being rude just now, Gwen, what do you call what you're doing?"

"Rudeness, too. But it's a matter of principle with me."

"Your high-falootin' integrity is more a lack of living, Gwen," the reporter challenged. "Sure, he's killed in the line of duty, and where he's from, that's the kind of law that's respected. It's a chancy life, Gwen. It makes a man watchful, and a little lonely too I bet."

"Since he kills off anybody near him, I imagine it would be lonely," the girl snapped angrily. "Kane's an executioner."

"So's the man who shoots a rabid dog, Gwen."

"It's a case of definitions, then. Who's the dog with rabies? And what right does this man or any of us have to judge it?"

Randolph leaned back in his chair. "You're lucky never to've needed a man like Kane, Gwen. Once you're up against a rabid dog, then it's too late to say you've been suffering from delusion and you want Marshal Kane to come help you. You see, he's a tool just like a fire-wagon or a dose of your quinine."

"My tools are used for constructive purposes, not destruction."

Kane sombrely plucked her hand from his sleeve. "I've had just about enough dissection from you for tonight. Whatever you think I am or have become, I'm a man who casts a shadow, Doctor Arling, and I've got my pride. I am not a specimen immune to your snide charges, and whether you excuse me or not, I'm going."

With that, the furious marshal spun on his heel and stalked out of the salon. Behind him the blushing Gwen Arling was trembling slightly with pent-up emotion. Randolph looked at Kane's retreating back, then up at her. He said: "You asked for that one, Gwen."

"Yes. . . . Yes, Irving, I suppose I did."

"I only hope that if or when you have to ask for help, he'll give it."

4

The boat trip stretched on endlessly for Kane, scraping his nerves more with each passing day. The ship became a plush-lined jail cell for him, and meal-time was a marshland of unfamiliar food and etiquette which never failed to nauseate him. His only solace was, strangely enough, Irving Randolph. After that horribly embarrassing evening when Randolph first recognized him, Kane had slowly discovered that Randolph was not interested in cheap-jack promotion. Randolph had gone out of his way to apologise to him for Dr Arling's spirited behaviour, and then invited him to a private card game where the whiskey flowed and the betting was high calibre, but for low stakes. A gentlemen's game, played by men who knew what the hell they were doing. Kane enjoyed himself thoroughly one late evening, and managed to relax in Randolph's company after that.

"Give me a machine to transcribe my words," Randolph told him, "and I'll set fire to the world with my thoughts."

"Just so long as it's not thoughts about me, that's fine," Kane replied. He made it clear he wished to stay as anonymous as possible, and Randolph promised to honour the wish. "Your life is a fascination, but I'll give it my discretion for now."

Occasionally Kane would meet the lovely Doctor Arling, though he never sat with her for dinner after their first introduction. She was constantly in the company of her older colleague, Dr Schwartz, and two nurses, Miss Hall and Miss Prentice. Dr Schwartz spoke with a thick Germanic accent, rolling his Rs and making his vowels into guttural sounds.

On the eleventh day of the journey, an incident happened which threw Dr Arling and Kane together again, much against their desires.

Kane was passing through the deck lounge, and absently smiled at a pretty young girl who was sitting beside a drunken older man. The girl smiled back, and the man took offence, saying something under his breath which obviously insulted her. She reared back and slapped his face. With a snarl, the drunk man whipped up a fist to hit her—and then Kane took charge. Partially out of boredom, partially out of frustration and because the girl was cute and didn't need to be hit, Kane defended her harder than he need have. He shoved the man's face into the sliced pineapple that was on the table in front of them. Then he continued on walking as if nothing had transpired.

The girl squeaked: "Oh look out!"

Kane weaved to one side, barely ducking a heavy glass ashtray the man had sent sailing directly for his head. As it was, one corner cut into the crown of his head, tearing skin and raising blood. Kane tottered backward, trying to catch his balance as the drunkard came swinging. Kane bobbed from one hamhanded roundhouse blow, then caught the next, twisted it around in the palm of his hand, and then sunk his own fist into the man's belly. The man's eyes bulged out, rancid breath bellowing from his lungs, and Kane let go to see him flop, writhing, to the deck. Kane looked down, breathing hard, ignoring the blood which rivuleted from his scalp. He heard tapping footsteps and thought it was the girl approaching, but when he glanced across, he saw that the girl had vanished. Dr Arling was rushing toward him and the fallen man.

"You'll live," she said tersely after glancing quickly at Kane's wound, and then knelt by the drunk.

Kane, trembling with rage, snatched up a napkin and pressed it to his face. He left in a trail of waiters, went straight to his cabin and a bottle of whiskey.

Randolph came up to Dr Arling just as Kane was leaving. "Don't bother with that rabble, Gwen. Kane's got a bad cut."

Gwen Arling didn't reply, turning the unconscious man over and beginning to give him artificial respiration.

"Gwen—"

"I told that man that he'd live. This man might not."

"Nonsense. Kane merely knocked him out."

"I saw that blow, Irving. It was directly to the solar plexus as hard as he could hit. A great deal of internal damage can be done by such a blow. Believe me, I know. I'm the doctor."

A few minutes later, the drunk came to, grey of face and gasping for breath. His first words called for a drink.

"Well?" Randolph asked sarcastically, "Will he live?"

"No thanks to your friend, the marshal."

"Oh, cut it out, Gwen! Kane was only defending himself."

"He tried to kill this man with his fist, Irving." Dr Arling snatched up her bag then, her lips like white lines. "Now, Irving, I'll see to your friend's scalp wound."

"How generous of you, my dear."

Gwen Arling stalked out the same door Kane had exited through, asking one of the stewards to direct her to Kane's cabin. When she reached it, she knocked on the louvred door, asking if she could come in. There came a curt acceptance. She walked in, glaring coldly at Kane, who was slouched on the bed drinking whiskey out of the bottle. Blood had coagulated in clots and streams, giving his face a yet more sinister appearance. She went directly to the wash basin, where she began scrubbing her hands.

"What's all this for?" he asked warily.

"I'm a doctor, remember?"

"Just give me a piece of sticking plaster, lady."

"I am a *doctor,* Marshal Kane, and please don't forget it. It isn't anything but common-sense precaution against infection."

She came over and sat down beside him, washing away the dried blood. "Clean, but. . . . I'm going to have to sew."

Kane grunted something under his breath.

"Tell me if you're going to faint," she said to him, taking out a sterilized needle and catgut thread. "Most of them do."

"Do what? Tell or faint?"

"Don't be funny, it doesn't become you." She

moistened the cut with rubbing alcohol, making Kane grit his teeth against the acutely stinging pain. But he'd be damned if he'd show her one tiny wince! She began sewing, and he had two choices: stare at her breasts that were almost rubbing his face, or up at her face. He decided to focus on her eyes, her breasts being too much a temptation. When she finished, he still hadn't moved. Coldly, she said:

"You can have a drink now."

"Thanks—*lady.*"

She stiffened at the casual insult. The piece of adhesive she'd placed over her stitching gave him a menacing pirate's black eyepatch look now. She felt something inside her stirring against her will, responding to the basic animal brutality of this man. She quickly turned away, repacking her satchel bag. "Don't touch the bandage," she told him brusquely. "I'll take it off along with the stitches in about a week. The scar should be nearly invisible."

"It'll suit the others," Kane said with indifference. "How much do I owe you for your emergency service?"

"Nothing. It's called help, Marshal Kane. H-E-L-P. Ever heard of the word before?"

He swore at her as she walked out the cabin door.

She removed the stitches six days later, again using his cabin as her operating theatre. She washed the mostly healed wound with antiseptic, then fastened a much narrower strip of plaster.

"Still nothing to pay?" Kane asked with a satiric smile.

"Nothing," she repeated firmly, and left.

Whenever he saw her now, she was in turgid discussions with Dr Schwartz, strictly ignoring Kane on any basis except doctor-patient. Damn snooty bitch, Kane thought when seeing her. Pretty woman and she knows it, dressing in conservative dresses so that her obvious curves wouldn't be a distraction. But they distracted Kane nonetheless, and he often had sultry daydreams about her when he was lying in his cabin alone, drinking beer. It was her animosity which attracted him; the challenge that her overt contempt for him caused Kane to respond to instinctively. The attraction was a danger as far as he was concerned. Kane considered it a weakness, and watched sharply for any signs that conditions might warm between them. Gwen Arling was not the type to love and leave in a one-night fling—any more than Kate Coleman had been—and getting involved with wildcat prideful bitches like her or Kate was the ruin of any man.

The night before docking, he again asked her if she was *sure* there was no payment. Somewhat to his surprise, she gazed at him with her cool grey eyes and said yes, since he insisted, he might pay her ten dollars. The ten-dollar bill Kane gave her went into her bag, to be used, she told him, to buy quinine.

Whatever victory Kane might have felt then, turned bitter like the taste of quinine itself.

Days later, Gwen Arling was merely a small thorn in Kane's pride. He stood in the foyer of the chandelier-lit ballroom, thinking of more important matters than the cool snub of that haughty girl. There was, after all, the over-riding pressure of his assignment, which had begun the moment he'd debarked from the boat in Colon. A liveried driver, waiting with a polished black carriage, had intercepted him on the dock, introducing himself as being from the consul, who'd like to meet him at once.

Time was pressing, Kane was told; the consul was dining in a short while with the British ambassador and wouldn't be available afterwards.

Kane enjoyed the quick-trotting ride from the busy port. The carriage passed through the Central American drowsiness, breaking into the mass of yelling French voices, armies of sweating mulattos, and swarms of dusky natives and mixed-blooded mestis. The carriage continued upward into the finer residential district, toward a green ridge covered with *palmetto* where a low, white house in the Spanish style nestled in the dwarf palms' shade.

Another servant opened the door, and guided Kane through the cool corridors of the house. He stood aside for Kane to enter a large panelled office, shutting the door silently behind Kane. A tubby man with thick-veined cheeks and piercing eyes stood up from a large desk across the room. He extended a hand, introducing himself. "I'm Michael Cleaver, Mr Kane. Welcome."

Kane sat down next to the desk after shaking hands. The consul continued speaking. "I've taken the liberty of reserving a room for you at the Presidential, one of the better hotels in this madhouse town. When we're finished, I'll have you driven down to it. I'm sorry we won't have much time, but as my chauffeur may have explained, I've a pressing engagement very shortly. But first, won't you have a drink?"

The "drink" was one of an endless series of glasses filled with gin and lemon juice. Kane, who rarely drank anything but whiskey, was leery of the concoction at first, but discovered why it was one of the most popular drinks in the area, when one cool sip quenched his thirst without the burning rawness of whiskey. It was an excellent fighter of the climate, and by the look of the consul, he'd been waging a long and successful campaign with it. For three-quarters of an hour, Kane mostly sat and drank, listening to the consul expound on the local troubles.

"Four, perhaps five miles a day is all the canal is progressing, Mr Kane. The French haven't been able to manage it, it's quite clear they haven't, but frankly, I'm not sure anybody can at this point."

"Is Colombia causing trouble?"

"On the contrary, the government here is most anxious to see the canal succeed. It's a money-maker for them. But the local residents are ferociously independent, and what's good for Colombia is automatically bad for Panama. I don't think their reasoning is sound—but then, when it comes to such nationalism, emotions take precedence over reason."

"Sabotage?"

"The Colombians have been quite good about guarding against sabotage. It sometimes looks as if there's one soldier for every worker. Thefts, though, that's a different case. Pilferage of anything that isn't nailed down, and no matter how conscientious the Colombians want to be, there's always some graft as well. I'm sure some of the guards are getting a rakeoff for turning a blind eye. Yes, theft and drunkenness all add to the problem."

"But they aren't the main problem, is that it?"

The consul shook his head. "It's my opinion that the French aren't going to succeed for two basic reasons. One is disease. Until a cure and, more importantly, a prevention is found for the fevers down here, sickness will wipe out too many good men. Also, I don't believe the machinery has been invented yet that can properly do the job. It will in time, but not in time for this particular project." The consul drew a long sip on his drink, then sighed and sat back thoughtfully. "You know, Mr Kane, there's one other small item that's just cropped up which might bear watching."

"What's that?"

"Oddly enough, a large number of labourers from our American project in Nicaragua are down here looking for work."

"They've deserted us?"

"I . . . don't know. In a sense they have, because they're down here and not up working in Nicaragua, but they keep swearing that they've been promised jobs on the Panamanian project. And for the astronomical wage of twenty-five dollars per month. I'd think it was the *pinga* getting to their brains, except that they all say it, drunk or sober, and they seem to actually believe it. Of course I can't blame them for leaving us up in Nicaragua to come here if that's the case. I mean, that's a twenty dollar raise."

"I'll keep that in mind when I get up to Nicaragua," Kane said.

"Yes, do that. Will you be staying in Colon long before travelling on, Mr Kane?"

"I'll be moving just as soon as possible."

"I advise going by coastal steamer. Ride up to the San Juan del Norte, then along the river. You'll meet the canal workers. They haven't reached any further inland than the French, to be frank about it. Stories of terror, fires. . . . Rumours, more'n likely, but I tell you I'm worried nevertheless."

"Well, that's what I'm going to find out."

"Be sure you watch out for bandits as well, Mr Kane. Whatever you do, don't take a trip by yourself;

those cut-throats seem to be able to smell a victim and kill without blinking an eye."

"I'll keep that in mind, too."

"But before you go, you will come to a reception I'm holding, won't you? Later on tonight, after the ambassador and so forth—which is why I couldn't see you on business except now."

"It'd sure beat sitting alone in my room."

"Fine, then I'll have you called for at, say, nine-thirty?"

"That'll be fine."

"Perhaps we'll find more time to talk, party or no. . . ."

Now, standing stiffly in his finest clothing, Kane glanced around the glittering throng of the reception. He wasn't so sure he should have accepted the consul's invitation, and would probably have preferred to remain inconspicuous in his own plain garb, eating a local meal and speaking in Spanish to the natives. In that respect, Kane felt more at home than with his own Americans—it was a matter of position, not of nationality. Yet Kane had sensed that the consul's request was a lightly veiled command, and he figured he'd only be making a potential black mark on his new record if he failed to make an appearance. Besides, the consul just might be able to pass on some more information tonight.

In a few more hours Kane would be neck deep in tropical growth, fighting snakes and disease and machete-swinging bandits. This respite might be his last in a long time, he thought, and he might as well enjoy it for what it was worth. He started toward the champagne punchbowl, then paused, staring across the crowded ballroom. Christ, it was a jungle in here, too! Coming nearer was Gwen Arling, gorgeously svelte in a low-cut red gown.

He smiled at her, baring his teeth. "Good evening, Doc. Warn me if there're any ashtrays flying, will you . . . ?"

5

The heat was oppressive, but not as bad as the humidity, which was a solid clammy pressure stifling the body and lungs. Kane panted from the mugginess, and wished he was back in the pleasant surroundings of Colon, where at least the coastal breezes tempered the hot weather. Here, inland on the San Juan River, there was no relief from the ever-present heat and dampness.

The river meandered along a low, sandy tongue of land; through lowlands where natives cultivated maize, bananas, cocoa and hemp, toward the distant towering ridges of fertile jungle. Because the river had waterfalls and cataracts, the steamer was unable to navigate as far as Kane had to go; he'd been forced to hire a canoe rowed by two Indians. The Indians spoke a pidgin Spanish and seemed to live on bananas, cocoa-leaves, and rum. Kane loathed bananas and hated cocoa-leaves. Which made the rum look like the best alternative, and for the two nights it'd taken them to paddle upriver, he'd sat around with them sipping the liquor out of an earthenware jug.

The rum helped him to sleep. It seemed as if the

setting of the sun was a sort of signal for every screeching bird, howling animal, and buzzing insect to wake up and make life a noisy misery for him. His mosquito net fairly bulged inward from the weight of the humming bastards eager to needle him. And no sooner would he drift off, than the sky would abruptly open up with a monsoon, drenching him for five sodden minutes, then disappear as quickly as it'd begun. Kane was forced to lie in steaming bedclothes under the netting, hearing the hollow roll of rainwater off the trees and shrubs add to the racket of the fauna.

Frequently he'd recall that reception given by the consul, Michael Cleaver. And how Dr Arling had looked so ravishing in her gown, smiling with a light laugh when he'd spoken to her. She hadn't stayed for conversation then, however, whirling on among the throng of important personages—the diplomats, the engineers, even de Lessup himself, father of the Panama canal project. De Lessup was a small man with a black goatee and a nervous air like an impatient martyr. He was talking to a toad-like man whom he introduced to Kane as Monsieur Kanter, the project's Director of Security.

"A hard job?" Kane had asked to start conversation flowing.

"M'sieur, the natives would steal the shirts off our backs if given the opportunity," Kanter said in fluent English. "A primitive mob, sir, absolutely stone-age in their concepts."

"M'sieur Kanter has just returned from an inspection trip to Colon," de Lessup explained. "He's a bit short of patience with some of the pilfering going on, and. . . . Ah! Franz! Come here, Franz and meet M'sieur Kane. M'sieur Kane, Franz Streicher."

A thin, sunburnt man was introduced. Kane noted the telltale bulge of a concealed pistol inside Streicher's jacket. "My bodyguard," Kanter said, as if reading Kane's expression. "I must be the most detested man on the project, as you can imagine. Franz makes sure I don't earn a machete in the neck or a bullet in the back for my efforts. The last security director was cut in half when he caught a gang of thieving Indians."

Streicher didn't change his expression, regarding Kane with cool precision. "And you, Mr Kane?"

"And me?"

"What is your position with our company?"

"None. I'm merely passing through on my way to Nicaragua, and Mr Cleaver was kind enough to extend an invitation for tonight."

"Ah, then you're part of your American canal project."

"Not really," Kane answered with care. "Just looking around."

"Aren't we all," Kanter said with dark amusement. "Aren't we all. . . ." He was smiling as he turned to stare at Dr Arling's full breasts, their rich upper portion bare in her tight red dress. Streicher seemed to turn away, as if repelled—Kane wondered why. Was Streicher anti-woman, or did he dislike his boss' crude leering glance? A strange pair, he decided inwardly. . . .

"Do you dance, Mr Kane?"

Kane glanced at Gwen Arling, surprised that she'd spoken to him at all, much less asked for a dance. "Not if I can help it. Perhaps some exercise in the form of walking?" He gestured toward the open doors leading to the villa's garden.

"That sounds pleasant—but so does the music.

I'm afraid I'll have to postpone our walk at least until I've had this dance with that dashing Colombian colonel. Isn't he beautiful?"

Kane was even more shocked by her use of the word "beautiful" to describe a soldier. But examining the man, Kane could see Gwen's point: he was bronze-skinned, black-eyed, waxed moustached, bemedalled and be-ribboned, pleated and sashed and full of ornate curlicues on his layers of uniform. "Oh he's adorable," Kane grumbled under his breath as the colonel approached.

"Meet Colonel Jose de Jesus y Correida de Valparaiso," Gwen said in one breath. "Colonel of the local garrison in Panama. Colonel Valparaiso, this is Mr Kane."

"At your service," the Colonel said, bowing and clicking his heels. "And now, señorita . . . ?" He extended an arm, leading Gwen onto the dance floor and into a stately waltz.

Kanter chuckled. "A clown, eh?"

De Lessup looked irritated at his security director. "We shouldn't give Mr Kane here the impression that we consider the Colombian army foolish. Actually they are very capable and brave men, iron disciplined and—"

"Greedy as hell," Kanter interrupted.

"You're imagining things," de Lessup snapped back. "I suppose that's your nature or you wouldn't be in charge of security, but still, it's not particularly fair to make such gross remarks."

"Not without proof, eh?" Kanter said slyly, and then moved on before de Lessup could respond. Kane frowned, wondering what Kanter knew—if only by intuition and experience. He'd all but called the Colonel a corrupt numbskull.

Kane was still pondering the point and hoping to be able to talk to Kanter alone before leaving, when Gwen approached him for that walk in the garden. Kane pushed aside his curiosity about Kanter and the Colonel, guiding her with one hand out the doors and along the moonlit path. She was along purely out of politeness, Kane surmised; she couldn't stand him, not really, and she still irked him as well. This was a ploy of manners, not of affection.

Then she said in a most sincere voice: "I must apologise."

"What?"

"I'm sorry, Mr Kane, for the way I acted on the boat."

"You *treated* me very well," he replied, touching his forehead.

"Yes, but I acted atrociously. Irving has talked to me since then, and has told me a great deal about you. I was biased against you—I still am, I suppose—but that's no excuse."

"Forget it," Kane said curtly, wanting to avoid the subjects of himself, what Randolph might know about him, or what she may think of him because of it. "Tell me, where are you going next?"

"Inland. It's our intention to build a mobile clinic that'll move along with the canal project. Colonel Valparaiso will be helping; the Colombian government is funding the entire cost."

"A hard task."

"Yes, but I can't wait to get started. Just like you in your . . . line of work." She paused on the pathway, looking up into his eyes with determination. "You say you're going to Nicaragua, and Randolph keeps talking about all the bloodshed and sabotage that's going on up there. Be careful, Mr Kane."

"I plan to. But . . . why this sudden about-face?"

She smiled wistfully, averting her eyes and gazed back into the well-lit ballroom. "Did you hear that Mr Kanter speak about how low the natives are? Corrupt, lazy, good-for-nothing . . . I come from Virginia, Mr Kane, and we talk about our negroes in about the same terms, as if they're some sort of subhuman species, hardly better than dumb animals. Prejudice, Mr Kane, that's all it is whether it's a Southerner talking about his 'nigger', or Mr Kanter castigating the workmen, and I dislike bigotry in anybody. I particularly despise it in me, and I'm afraid that I jumped to conclusions about you all too soon. Prejudice, Mr Kane. I don't believe in those things I took you to task for, and I don't feel right in blaming you for them quite so soon. You see now?"

"I see." Kane looked with her toward the villa. The Colonel was coming outside onto the patio, his sword clanking against his pantleg. For a moment he was silhouetted in the light—then a shot rang out. The Colonel fell to a crouch, yelling: "Attack!"

Kane was already running toward him as the shot's noise died away. Streicher was approaching as well, his stubby pistol in hand. "Are you hurt?"

The Colonel got up warily, brushing his knees. "No, no."

Kane stopped, relieved to see that the Colonel wasn't wounded. Gwen reached his side, breathing heavily, her hands tight around his arm. "Oh my God," she gasped. "How horrible."

Kane glanced at her, smiling to himself. She'd reverted to being a frightened woman in the first seconds of shock and fear—in another minute, she'd become Doctor Arling again, efficiently checking over the Colonel, but it was enough for Kane to know that inside her, there was a feminine quality that hadn't been buried successfully. Yet.

"Did you see him?" Kane asked Streicher.

Streicher nodded. "Just a glimpse. An Indian jumping over the low gate there and heading for the brush. It had to be him."

"I'm almost getting used to it," Valparaiso said with a cold smile. "These tiny anarchist groups—and I emphasise they are tiny—are a motley crew who'd do most anything for attention. I'm sure they picked this time and place on purpose, simply to embarrass and demonstrate. Well, they failed again, as always."

"Failed or not," de Lessup said, coming up beside the Colonel, "I'll personally complain to the governor. Absolutely scandalous!"

"Governor Heredia can't do any more than he is already," Valparaiso said in a calming tone. "Please, entrust this with me. I know how to handle such situations, and one of the very first rules is don't give them the attention they're seeking."

"Yes, yes maybe you're right. . . ."

Gradually the shocked and terrified guests calmed down, the waiters continued passing drinks, and the orchestra started playing again. Soon it was as if nothing had happened, at least superficially. Consul Cleaver took Kane aside, seeking a private chat. "Just between us," he said, "I should have liked that bullet to've nicked the Colonel just a little bit."

"Really?"

"Oh, I don't mean fatally. I mean enough to deflate his swelled head, is all. By God, he's an arrogant devil, and cruel. On the other hand, I'm glad for the natives he wasn't killed. Six months ago there was a state of emergency declared here in Colon. The Colombian soldiers posted here aren't from this region, and hate the people, so you can imagine just how summary and brutal the courts-martial were. Damn, what a turmoil! It'll blow sky-high one of these days. Mark my words, Kane, Panama is brewing for a major revolt . . ."

The consul moved away in search of a glass. Kane stood contemplating his remarks, his thoughts interrupted by Kanter coming up and speaking: "Odd, Mr Kane. Very odd, don't you think?"

"Perhaps. Your lifeguard is very effective, though."

"That's his job. I'm sorry Streicher couldn't bring the man down, but nobody's a perfect shot. The Indian was dashing through the darkness, and running out of a lighted room makes aiming at a target very difficult."

"You don't have to apologise for him, Mr Kanter."

"No, I know I don't. I suppose I'm mostly reassuring myself." He smiled wryly. "After all, it could've been me just as well as Colonel Valparaiso that the bullet was meant for. I'm just damn glad de Lessup insisted I have a bodyguard at all."

Kanter wandered back in among the guests, as Cleaver had done before him. Again Kane was alone, but again, not for long. Gwen Arling came up to him, with Colonel Valparaiso in tow. "It's late for me, and I'll be going," she said. "I wanted to say goodbye, Mr Kane. Good luck, and . . . do take care."

"Thank you. Is Colonel Valparaiso seeing you to your hotel?"

She smiled. "If that's an oblique offer, Mr Kane, it's very sweet of you. But I'm afraid as *Doctor* Arling, I'm seeing the Colonel to his quarters. I'm sure you understand?"

The Colonel flashed a toothy, fatuated grin at Kane as they turned around to find their host and say goodnight. Kane felt irritated beyond measure for a number of reasons. One, because he'd stepped out on the social limb and made a play for the girl, after swearing he'd never do it. Two, because she seemed to read through his turmoil and found it amusing enough to smile. Three, because she declined. And four, because that tinplated comic-opera Colonel had her for himself tonight. Some tough soldier!

But then, as he thought about it a second time, he saw the humour in the situation. If he'd been in the soldier's boots, he'd have done the exact same thing, no doubt. Coming down with an abrupt case of wounded nerves or sprained ego, or whatever it took to talk the lovely doctor into attending to him. Yeah, and with any sort of luck, in trying a little therapy of his own on her, too!

And now, lying on the soggy ground under the mosquito net, Kane recalled how he'd smiled thinly as he'd watched the couple leave the reception. And once again, he burst out laughing. It was the sort of black irony, the grim jest on human nature that appealed to his otherwise humourless character.

6

The Nicaraguan canal was a vast project, stretching almost a thousand feet alongside the river and promising to stretch a great deal further before it was through. Down in the shadowed depths of the long ditch, workers were swarming like moles in a wheel-rut, using wheelbarrows, pickaxes, drills, hammers and shovels to chew out the earth and spit it up into massive crude wagons for haulage. Two steam shovels and a steam engine were standing empty, ignored and pitted with rust. Kane didn't know why the engines weren't being used, nor how the hell those monsters ever got down into the ditch in the first place.

Kane paid his two Indian guides, gripped his bag and stepped up a weedy path to a low workman's hut which overlooked the digging site. He could see four white men standing around a sawhorse table, discussing blueprints. Before he could reach them, two armed negroes stepped forward, menacing him with their rifles.

Kane told them he had an appointment with the chief engineer.

One of the guards went over to the quartet, and they looked over to where Kane stood waiting. A squat, dirty man with a bristly beard waved Kane over, sticking out a ham-sized hand to be shook. "Put 'er there, Kane, we heard you were coming. Meet Hardy Villiers, Krueger, and Schlesinger. Me, I'm Malcolm Houston, the chief 'geer around here. Just call me Mel for short; all my friends do."

Kane greeted them in turn, grinning now from the warm welcome and infectious smile of Mel Houston. "Heard you were coming," he'd said; so Washington must've had this job up its sleeve for some time! Kane's old suspicions from back in Fort Leavenworth were now confirmed.

"We sure could've used you last week," Houston said. "Look at those engines over there. Hardly more'n scrap. It'll take months to get replacement parts down here for them."

"Sabotaged, eh?" Kane asked.

"No two ways about it. Boilers exploded and cylinders hammered to shreds. And that's not all: our main storage shed was blasted apart, setting afire most of our oil and grease supplies."

"Yeah, I'd like to've been here a week ago, alright," Kane said tersely. "But believe me, I got here quick as I could. Left the same day I got the assignment, less'n two weeks ago."

"You made good time," Villiers assented. "We're not blaming you, Kane; stuff like this has been going on a lot longer than just one week. C'mon in the shack and have some rum. . . ."

A half-hour later, Kane was educated in some of the ways the canal was being slowed. Foremen having their heel tendons cut, and too scared to describe who'd done it. Others sullenly picked fights and deserted under some false impression they could make five times as much in Panama, and nothing the white men could say could change their minds. Supplies were purposely being ruined, food was left to spoil, water contaminated . . . and always the fever took its own deadly toll. The project had only one doctor and two male orderlies to handle the increasing number of sick Indians, and the Indians refused what medical aid that was offered.

"Hell, we even have to disguise the quinine in batches of rum before they'll drink it," Krueger bemoaned.

"Don't you get any help from the Nicaraguan government?"

"The sort of help we don't need, Kane," Houston answered bitterly. "A company of dead-drunk guards who spend their duty down in the shanty town, whoring it when they're not unconscious. The soldiers are native Indians pressed into service, given old muzzle-loaders, half a uniform, and a kick in the ass. The officers are all political appointees, sons of landowners and such like. Useless bastards, soaking us for three hundred dollars a month. When we complain to the government in Managua, we get a reply back that the force is all they can spare because of border unrest. That is, when they feel like sending a reply at all."

"And we have to keep them," Villiers added. "That's part of our agreement with Nicaragua, and besides, if we didn't pay the officers, then they'd conveniently see that the soldiers deserted."

"They've already hinted at it," Schlesinger said, spitting into one corner. "With the soldiers gone, we'd be sitting ducks for the bandits hiding up in the hills, who're just waiting for an easy chance. Though God knows it's easy as it is, them chocolate troopers turning their backs to thieving with their palms outstretched."

"So they're being paid coming and going," Kane murmured, half to himself, "and doing it while sitting on their asses."

"Right."

"How many whites are there, Mel?"

"We four, three machinists, one with malaria, and the doc and his orderlies. None of us have time to play copper, though we've managed to build a private militia with some left-over rifles and some of the more trustworthy natives. Ten men in all—and they've got their hands out like the soldiers."

"What about the storage sheds?" Kane asked.

"We lock away what we can," Schlesinger answered. "But with a project of this size, we've got acres of supplies to protect. You see, Kane, it's pretty hopeless. We can't do it, and one man like yourself can't pull miracles out of a hat, either."

"Mm," Kane said, pursing his lips and frowning in thought. "Mm. . . . How far away is the capital from here?"

"Two days by boat, only our one steamer ran aground on Ometepe island, out in Lago de Nicaragua. So it's two weeks by foot."

"Good."

"Good!" The four engineers stared at Kane.

"I think I might have an idea. . . . Who's head of the guards?"

"A lieutenant named Sebaco," Schlesinger said. "All pearly teeth and bowing and scraping, as phony as a three-dollar bill. I wouldn't put it past him to've been the one who dynamited us."

"He hasn't the guts." Villiers argued.

"But the longer he stays the more money he gets from us. Besides, it couldn't have been any of the workers, they don't even know what dynamite is, much less how to work it. And we keep that stuff under lock and key like it's in a bank vault."

Kane studied Schlesinger, noting how his sharp blue eyes narrowed as he talked, and his thin lips compressed almost brutally. He said: "Alright, we're going to impress your Lieutenant Sebaco. Have you any fancy stationery around here? You know, full of fretwork and scrolls and stuff like that?"

"The company letterhead," Houston suggested. "I think we've got a few pieces still floating around that aren't too mouldy."

"I'll need a very solemn, officious letter written in Spanish."

"Kane, what on earth—?"

"You'll see. You get me the paper and I'll dictate. . . ."

A shabby mule carried Kane back down the hill some hours later, ambling in its weary way toward the project's shanty town. Inside Kane's jacket pocket was the carefully worded letter, dried over a kerosene lamp to give it a parchment texture. There was a little soot on it, but not enough to count. What did count was that Kane was no longer merely "Señor," but was now promoted to Colonel of the United States Armed Forces, appointed to assist the canal company's security detail, and nominated to similar standing in the Nicaraguan Army. There was a great many "therefores" and "whereases" in the letter, signed with illegible scrawls by all four engineers in their capacities as Secretary of State, the Ambassador to Nicaragua, Commander-in-Chief of the Nicaraguan Army, and a few more illustrious titles thrown in for good measure.

It was truly a *letter*. Kane was counting on it and his own slight knowledge of the armed services to bluff his way through. He was already angry enough to be a soured colonel, his straw hat pulled down low, a peevish straight line to his mouth, his eyes as dark and shiny as the revolver belt slung low across his hips.

The shanty town was a running sewer, adding injury to his insult. The shacks and tents were alive with drunk men, screaming children and yammering woman, all of them ignoring the only signs of military there were—six ragged soldiers slopping through the gummy mud, leaning on one another and singing in slurred Spanish. Kane reached the military post, which was hardly any better than the wooden-crate shacks of the civilians, and dismounted with all the authority he could muster. He stomped inside, confronting a startled orderly by banging a fist down on the one table in the room.

"Lieutenant Sebaco," he barked. "On the double!"

The orderly jumped a foot, then backed through a curtain into the rear of the cabin. Kane followed on his heels, elbowing the orderly aside when he saw his quarry, dressed in a lieutenant's dirty red jacket, encrusted with the spangles and slashes of his rank. His filthy white pants were off, exposing thin wiry legs. He was springing off a narrow bed when Kane entered, eyes wide with surprise, half bowling over a naked girl who'd been under him only seconds before. The girl opened her mouth to scream, then thought the better of it when Kane bellowed:

"An outrage, Lieutenant! How dare you!"

"Who are you to—"

"Shut your weasel's mouth, Lieutenant! And stand at attention when addressing your superiors. I want to see a snappy salute!"

Sebaco, still off guard and crimson from embarrassment, saluted out of habit. Kane's roaring voice had that bite of authority, even though he wasn't in a prescribed uniform. Sebaco was handed the fancied-up letter.

"Sir—"

"Can you read as well as you can make love?"

"Colonel Kane, I—"

"Shut up!" Kane snatched the letter away. "Get on your uniform, Sergeant, at once."

"I'm Lieutenant—"

"You will be Sergeant Sebaco in thirty seconds if you're not fit to be seen in twenty. Do you understand?" Kane took hold of the orderly and frog-marched him out of the back room. He shook the frightened soldier, raging: "Drink! Give me something to drink before I jam my boot in your ass so hard I knock out your teeth from inside!"

He slewed all the papers off the orderly's table and sat down in the orderly's chair. The orderly was scampering around witless, trying to find a bottle of something worth serving a colonel. He found one with a label and set it down with a glass, withdrawing all atremble and almost falling over the girl, who was slinking out from the rear room in her gunnysack dress. Kane gave her an appreciative smile. "Hey, hey señorita, what's your name?"

"Chilita, señor Colonel. I'm a virgin."

"I jus' bet you are," Kane chuckled, watching her trim little buttocks wriggle as she walked out the door. Then he scowled down at the glass. There was a dead cockroach in it. With a snarl, he threw the glass up in the air, drew his pistol and blasted the glass into smithereens. "A *clean* glass, you idiot!"

The orderly was nearly fainting by now. The room was filled with smoke, when Lieutenant Sebaco came hopping in with one leg still out of his trousers. "What was that? What was that?"

"Your *cojones*, Lieutenant!" Kane barked. "Atten-*chun*!"

Sebaco snapped to attention, saluting. His pants fell down.

"Now, there's going to be some new orders around here."

"Excuse me, Colonel," Sebaco quavered. "Excuse me but before new orders are given, even by you, I must have clearance from my immediate superior."

"And where is he?"

"In Managua, Colonel."

"Then I am closer, eh? Then I am more immediate than he!"

"Sir—"

"You don't like it? Perhaps you don't believe me? Fine! Go to Managua, Lieutenant, that's my very first order."

"Sir, it's at least fifteen days marching—"

"So you march, soldier! You march and complain and see where it gets you. Right back here to me, Lieutenant, right back here under my orders. And quite likely under a new lieutenant's orders by then, too. Yes, I think the walk would do you good."

"On reconsideration, Colonel, Sir, I am sure you're right."

"Right about the march?"

"Right about you being my immediate superior officer."

"Indeed. Very well, then to the new orders. A new form of payment will be instituted immediately. You and your men will be paid according to your worth. *After* achievement!"

There came a choking wail from the lieutenant. "Achievement?"

"Exactly! A bonus will be paid by the canal company for each arrest you make of the thieves and saboteurs. A very healthy bonus, do you understand?"

"Sir!" A crafty gleam was entering the Lieutenant's frightened eyes now. He could envision his choices: an exhausting trek to the capital, where he could complain and possibly overcome this infuriating ramrod Americano soldier; possibly—but then, the letter had looked very authentic, and he could get himself into more trouble than he was already, not only with the Colonel but with the brass at Managua. Or he could trust that the sizeable bonus was on the level and earn four weeks' pay instead.

When it came right down to basics, there wasn't much choice to make, he reasoned. "Colonel, your command is our wish!"

"Then get those drunken sops you call your patrol into some sort of order!" Kane roared at him. "At once! Dis-*missed*!"

Sebaco charged out of the shack, tripping over his pants and falling in the mud. Kane poured himself a hefty drink, using the sparkling glass the orderly had miraculously washed while he'd been dressing down the Lieutenant. Kane had difficulty not bursting with laughter, and concealed his amusement behind his drink.

Sebaco was a great deal busier for the next hour, and in as much righteous indignation as Kane had pretended to be. His two Second Lieutenants were dragged from various hovels and told in no uncertain terms that their mothers should have used contraceptives with the family goat, because look at the result. The Second Lieutenants skipped across the muddy squalor in search of their Captains, who received a similar lecture as to their heritage. Then the Captains searched out their Sergeants, repeating chapter and verse, who relayed it on to the regular troops.

Just before sunset, Kane led the entire crew at quick-march up the twisting trail to the engineers' encampment. When they reached the canal, their presence and disciplined order stopped work for half an hour, so awestruck were the labourers. Even the engineers were dumbfounded, staring silently at the parade. When Kane marched up and saluted, yelling: "Colonel Kane re-e-eporting as ordered!", Houston turned to Villiers and said, "No more rum for me, boy. I'm having hallucinations for sure."

Kane gave him a private wink and said under his breath: "Then save your bottle for me, Mel, because after I get these lunkheads set up for duty, I'll be wanting a drink. Damn, but all this crowing makes a man thirsty!"

7

A few days later, Kane lay sweating on the cot of the small shack he'd been given. Except for the insects, heat and humidity, he was fairly satisfied. The thefts had stopped. Each night a dozen rounds or so were fired by the soldiers, followed by a morning filled with miraculous tales of heroic defence against the bandits. Kane dutifully noted names and "bonuses" in a small book. Houston was glad to pay—it actually worked out less than the extortion he'd been paying Sebaco.

Kane conferred with the engineers every day—all except Schlesinger, who was rarely in the main camp. Schlesinger had a party of fifty Jamaicans working in an advance camp-site some distance upriver. Occasionally Kane visited the crudely built clinic, fashioned of palm fronds and corrugated iron plating. The young doctor there looked almost as bad as his patients, exhausted and verging on a breakdown from overwork. The victims of yellow fever and malaria were kept separated, as were the fewer cases of industrial accidents. Those with "yellow" sometimes vomited blood or oozed it right from the pores of their skin. They were doomed. The malaria cases were kept under mosquito netting, and the doctor remarked that the quinine reserves were just about used up. He'd ordered more from Managua, but so far nothing had come; pretty soon, he'd have to send a request to Panama and hope the French would sympathise even while competing.

The foremen with cut tendons were not in the clinic, since once their wounds had closed over, there was no more that could be done for them. Kane visited them, sickening with a black rage as he saw how pitifully the men crawled around, forced into slow, begging poverty. The foremen refused to help him, however. They wanted what lives they had left; humans were too cheap in Nicaragua for them to risk retaliation. But if he ever caught—

"Kane! Señor Kane!"

Kane swivelled from his cot, dashing through the door. An Indian was running toward him, waving his arms while trying to yell out his message. "Señor Kane, come quick! Shooting down at the canal! From the jungle, at the workers!"

"Wait a minute," Kane told the Indian, and ran back inside the hut for his pistol, belt, and straw hat. Then he followed the runner to the canal some distance away. He wasn't surprised he hadn't heard the shots; the noise of the construction would've covered them, the jungle swallowing anything else.

Now construction had halted, while workmen and foremen gathered around two dead men sprawled across their diggings. Just two unarmed labourers . . . and Kane could almost feel the strength of fear now in the others. Who'd be next? Houston was swearing. Villiers saw Kane, told Houston, who then called Kane to his side. "Out of nowhere," Houston snarled. "A crossfire from three snipers, way I can figure it, and then the skunks edged back away from the canal rim, into the jungle."

Villiers asked: "You want us to get the soldiers?"

Kane thought for a moment, then shook his head. "They'd go running around firing at everything, including themselves. No . . . but have you got a couple of reliable Indians?"

Villiers nodded, trotting over to where a foreman was staring down at the bodies. The foreman looked at Kane, then shouted something to two workers, who in turn came back with Villiers. Villiers explained: "The foreman's a brother of one of the slain men, and these two are cousins or something like that with the other. Both good in the brush, and trustworthy with guns."

"What're you planning to do, Kane?"

"Do a little smoking out, Mel, if I can. Got some rifles?"

Houston said: "Yeah, sure have," and led the way to one of the locked sheds. Inside he let Kane and the two Indians select from a rack of heavy Winchester 44/40 carbines. As he relocked the shed, the three huntsmen began moving swiftly in the direction the snipers had taken.

Plunging into the dense jungle gave Kane the creeps. The instant he stepped beyond the boundary of the project, it was as if he were enveloped in a thick, green tomb, and as they continued deeper into the growth, the more silent and oppressive it became. Trees rose so tall and thick that they blotted out the sun, rays only filtering through in oddly angled patches so that Kane couldn't take his bearings properly. He soon lost all sense of direction, for even the sound of the workmen was muffled and spread, echoing and re-echoing.

The Indians glided soundlessly across the moist turf, Kane hard pressed to keep up with their graceful speed. His revolverbelt gnawed at his hip, the rifle heavy as lead in his clammy grip, and his eyes stung with sweat. A cloud of insects swarmed around him, reminding him with their persistent bites that he'd forgotten to take quinine for a last few days.

The Indians stopped, placing fingers to their lips. Kane nodded, pausing as quietly as they. Then he motioned for them all to spread out, the Indians on either flank and Kane in the middle. Again they began to inch forward, and within minutes the jungle had swallowed the Indians. Kane felt absolutely alone and adrift. The rifle seemed as impractical as a cannon in this growth, he thought gloomily; the enemy could be hunkering down behind any tree or bush and he'd never know it till a machete cut his head off. It was all too silent, too closed-in for him. Christ, give him the wide-open plains, the dusty sand and dry heat of Arizona over this any day! He had no business down here at all.

A shot rang out, to be instantly sucked up by the jungle. Kane paused motionless, trying to orient its direction. Some leaves rustled nearby. He swivelled toward the new sound, but all was still again. Slowly he turned around with the carbine held ready, his eyes stinging and blurred, the nape of his neck tingling with fear. Then a third noise, like a soft sigh of a dying man, followed by a dull click as if a hammer had driven a nail into wood. He gripped his carbine harder—then let go of it, stepping back quickly, hair standing on end.

In the butt of the carbine, where it'd been nestling against his shoulder, was a thin poisoned dart. Another inch higher and he'd have been wearing it as a necklace! He stomped the dart free with his boot heel, then snatched up the carbine and began retreating into the foliage, crouching and trying to look in all directions simultaneously. The jungle was quiet . . . too quiet. . . .

Another rifle shot cracked out, sending a bird cawing from some far-off tree branch. Kane itched to empty the carbine into the surrounding green, but held back, forcing himself to get control of his senses. This was a new form of fighting, and he was frightened of it because of his inexperience. But if he hoped to get out of here with his skin intact, he'd damn well have to use cold calculation, not heated emotion. He waited, conditioning himself to this stalker's game of stealth and ambush.

Some nearby scrub whispered again, but not from any wind. There came a footstep. Kane hunkered lower, wondering if it were one of his Indians returning, but not about to stand up and take the chance of finding out too quickly. From out of the shadows crept an Indian—but not one of his, Kane immediately saw. This man had a long black beard and a loin-cloth wrapped like a diaper, his skin a darker hue. He was holding a long barrelled rifle in his left hand and a blowpipe in his right, and slung over one bare shoulder like a Sam Browne belt, was a small quiver of darts. The Indian moved closer. Kane sighted his rifle, all fear gone now as he felt the satisfaction of being the hunter instead of the hunted. He hesitated until there could be no possible mistake—than squeezed the trigger. The Indian went down with a crash.

Behind the first Indian was a second, hidden from Kane's view until now. The second Indian spun toward Kane, raising his blowpipe with all the tremendous speed and precision a life in the jungle forces upon a man. Kane levered and fired automatically, responding with the trained instincts of long years. He felt a breeze whistle past his left ear, and saw the Indian crumple atop his blowpipe, his chest blown apart by Kane's bullet.

Kane dropped to his knees again, tense and anxious in case yet another Indian and still more darts waited to fly at him. Nothing. Kane stayed put for another five minutes, but still there was no further sound or movement. Cautiously he reloaded his carbine and crept forward to the dead Indians. He kept well away from their quivers, but picked up the first Indian's rifle. It was a bolt-action Hotchkiss, designed by an American while in France and originally manufactured there.

How'd these natives get a weapon like this? Kane wondered.

And what had happened to his own allies? Kane put the rifle back down and crept stealthily to his left, hoping to intersect one of his comrades. Some seventy yards from where he'd started, he found the first Indian lying over his Winchester, most of his head had been blown away by a bullet. Kane shuddered involuntarily and retraced his steps, now going toward his right. The second Indian he eventually discovered propped against a tree, as if sleeping on the job. Only when Kane touched his shoulder, he slumped over into a heap. Protruding from his jugular was a dart.

Now Kane was *really* alone. Or was there a third enemy still lurking in the shadows, the last of the trio Houston supposed had killed the workmen? Kane didn't know, couldn't tell, his heart beating loud and fast. He only wanted to get out of this emerald green hell, but he couldn't even manage that—he didn't know how far or in what direction the canal lay! And twilight was coming, with its sudden lavender radiance and quick plunge into total blackness. Christ, how could he have gotten so twisted around?

He thought desperately for a few minutes, trying to figure out his best chance. It occurred to him that the skirmish had taken place while his Indians were on his flank, so that if he returned to where he'd fought and retraced his steps from there, he'd get back to where they'd initially parted company. He'd have to keep a straight line very carefully, however as just straying a bit would have him wandering forever in this jungle belt.

Anxiously he moved through the thick growth, concentrating on keeping the two dead Indians juxtaposed in his mind. Even so, he became lost, and only by accident stumbled across the two enemies he'd slain. With a sigh of relief, he then began working toward the spot where everybody had split up. It was dark by the time he reached it, and he realized that it was useless to continue. He'd have to spend the night in the jungle, then catch the first rays of the sun tomorrow morning for further directions.

He settled with his back to a large moss-covered tree. The sickly-sweet odour of orchids clogged his nostrils, and he felt queasy. And cold. Odd, he thought, to feel cold when it was so hot and he was sweating so much. He wondered if Houston was worried, or if the natives knew the jungle so well they could find him even in the dark. That'd be nice. He'd have to stay awake in case they came . . . Stay awake. . . .

Kane's head nodded with sleep.

He awoke with a start, blinking crusted eyelids apart. Over him were three black figures, and his initial thought was that they were from the project. He rose up, starting to smile, but then saw the closest one bring a machete around in a wild swing. He tried to twist away and grab his rifle, but it was as if he wasn't fully conscious yet; he wobbled off balance and his finger was clumsy on the carbine. Then the machete landed and Kane sunk to the soggy earth with a feeble groan, blank to the world.

He didn't know that he'd been hit over the head with the flat side of the machete blade, his last reaction being that of pure horror at the idea of having his head severed off. He snored raggedly, knocked out and dreamless, while the men disarmed him and tied his arms and legs with thongs. Then he was hefted over the shoulders of the strongest, and was carted like a sack of feed grain through the jungle. The loudest sound made was Kane's own breathing.

8

Kane rolled over, gradually becoming aware of the taste of dirt in his mouth. Heavy poundings were splitting his skull open, as if one of those steam shovels from the canal had taken root in his head.

Slowly his senses returned, though remained dull and painful under the constant ache between his eyes, and while spitting out the dirt, he could feel his mouth and throat dry and raw. The thirst grew insufferable along with his consciousness.

He tried to move, but only succeeded in rolling over again into the dirt. His hands were tied behind him, his ankles together and his legs bent up with the same long thong that was attached to his wrists. Whenever he tried to straighten out, he only managed to tighten the knots around his wrists and ankles. He wrestled futilely for awhile, then lay back panting, letting his headache weaken, until finally the realization dawned on him:

He was alive!

It seemed a strange notion to him, for his last recollection had been the savagely swinging machete aimed for his skull. He had no right to be alive, but this was surely no hellfire-and-brimstone purgatory. He was tied up solid, but he was breathing. And around him was the filthy dirt floor of a hut made of large stones and palm fronds. Through the chinks in the stones, he could see the outline of a clearing outside, and of a fire with three hunched men around it. Kane twisted about, searching for some way to escape, nausea sweeping over him along with pain. He stopped, having to lay still with his eyes closed until his head subsided and his dizziness passed, then glanced about again. More stone and palm leaves, and a length of rotted burlap cloth hanging down to act as a door. That was all.

Half crawling, half rolling, Kane inched toward the covered doorway. Panting with exhaustion and feeling sweat rivulet down his face, he lay while he listened to the three men outside. They weren't natives, but coal-black Jamaicans dressed in dirty cotton pants and jackets. Nearby within easy reach were their weapons—more bolt-action rifles and a brace of machetes, plus Kane's revolver and gun-belt. They spoke in a mixture of Spanish and Portuguese, tainted by their own dialect. He had to concentrate hard to catch any of the words at all: camp; river; scrub; *El Patron*, their boss. . . . None of it fit into a pattern sufficient for Kane to understand the gist of their conversation. After a few minutes he lost interest, squirming again with his intense need to free himself. By keeping his legs bent, there was a little slack in the thong attaching ankles and wrists; he bowed his back, straining with all his might, feeling a tiny stretching of the knot which held his wrists together.

Frequently Kane had to stop, too weak to continue. Gasping and sweating, he'd recoup his flagging strength before starting again, staring out between the rocks of the wall at the men and the campfire and the grey, false-dawn above the trees. He'd been unconscious most of the night, he figured, and soon it would be morning. His tongue felt swollen and caked, the slight musical sound of a creek trickling by on the other side of the clearing was like torture to his mind.

He kept working on the thongs with stubborn persistence, until the sky grew pearly and the negroes put out the campfire. One stood up, stretched, yawned, scooped up some food from a pot with a hollowed-out coconut shell, and started toward the hut. Kane wriggled back to where he'd been. The negro entered through the burlap, grunting with contempt as he saw Kane helpless on the ground. Kane almost vomited from the mere smell of the rancid food. The Jamaican thought this was funny, and grinning, squatted down to press the coconut shell under Kane's nose. He made a sign for Kane to open his mouth. Kane turned away, disgusted. The Jamaican scooped a handful of stew out and hit Kane in the face with it. Kane shuddered, opening his mouth to take the rest of the shell's contents, somehow forcing himself to chew the stringy meat and swallow the foul broth.

Coconut shell empty, the Jamaican rose and started back out. Kane called after him: "*Aqua*—water!" His voice was a feeble croak, and the negro didn't seem to take any notice of it. But a few minutes later the man returned with the coconut shell filled with brook water. He flung the entire bowl in Kane's face, laughed heartily, and left again. Kane licked his face as far as his tongue could reach, grateful for even the slightest drop of fresh water.

His three captors ignored him for the rest of the day. They went to the shade of some trees growing near the creek, brought up a jug of pinga that they'd evidently been cooling in its water, and settled down for some lazy drinking. Kane continued working on his bonds, increasingly frantic now as the minutes passed. He managed to stretch the thongs a little more—but not enough.

Around about noon, two native Indians came into the clearing. The Jamaicans called to them and there was a short conference, then the Indians left as silently and gracefully as they'd arrived. Kane couldn't hear what had been said, but he feared it was no good. The more he lay there, the more certain he became that he should have died the previous night. He was being kept a prisoner, and he didn't doubt that when he found out why and by whom, no mercy would be shown him. His wouldn't be a quick death under the swift blade of a machete. No, he'd obviously been lured into the jungle by the sniping attack on the canal, and his two Indian companions had been murdered so he alone would be taken. He had the morbid suspicion that he could've been just as easily killed yesterday if that had been part of the scheme. Instead, it had all been a trap—a trap laid by *El Patron*, who supplied his men with French-built rifles and knew exactly what Kane was up to and where to find him. It stunk, Kane thought. It stunk worse than that wretched stew the Jamaican had made him eat. It stunk all the way to Panama, he damn well suspected.

His single slim chance was to get loose. There was a good thirty feet of clearing between him and the weapons, which were still stacked next to the dead campfire. The Jamaicans were lounging with a fresh jug a few feet further on. If he got untied, Kane knew he'd have to reach the weapons before they could react, which would depend on how surprised and drunk they were. *If* he got untied. . . . By a fluke, his belt and holstered revolver were lying almost on top of the pile, and seeing it spurred Kane on. It was a tangible goal he could focus on, even if he got no further. But he'd rather die fighting on his feet, than as helpless sport for some brutal *El Patron.* Or perhaps left to live afterwards, with his Achilles tendons cut.

He tugged on the thongs, tugged until the pain was excruciating and blackness swam in front of his eyes. He thought his wrists would become disjointed, but the river of sweat streaming from his skin acted almost like a lubricant, softening the thin strips of hide and helping to make them pliant.

Slowly, like pulling a stubborn cork, he wrestled his right hand free.

The rest was simple, since the knots had been tied on the basis of mutual tension. He feverishly unravelled the thongs, crouching to rub circulation back into his wrists and ankles while peering between the stones to see exactly how he should attack the Jamaicans. Two were lying under the trees, unmoving. A third was standing beside the carcass of a monkey, stripping meat off its bones. The sight of the monkey's almost human paw made Kane quiver with nausea again. Coldness swept over him like he was in the Arctic instead of Central America, and he had to hold himself tight for some moments before his teeth stopped chattering. It wasn't the sight of the monkey that was causing it, he knew—but he didn't want to think about what it was. There wasn't time for it, not yet. Kane had more immediate business to attend. . . .

Now!

Kane charged from the hut in a crouching lope, heading straight for his revolver. He was half-way there when he was first noticed, a shout from the man cutting the monkey disturbed the others. There was a wild race for the weapons, Kane beating the Jamaicans to the pile by fractions of a second. He drew his pistol and threw himself in a flat leap to one side, firing at the monkey-carving negro just as a knife whizzed over his head. The negro staggered back against the monkey, a hole in his chest, clutching the hanging carcass as if for support, and dragging it down on top of him as he fell lifeless to the ground.

Kane was rolling, coming up to fire repeatedly. The second Jamaican tottered, throwing up the rifle he'd grabbed, and collapsed across the pile of weapons. The third still had the jug in one hand, a machete in the other. Eyes crazed, he suddenly turned and splashed across the creek in a vain attempt to escape. Kane blew part of his head off with no regrets, and the water ran red.

Weakly Kane stood up, surveying the carnage. It was very quiet now, only the sound of the water surging around the third corpse broke the calm aftermath. Kane bent and retched, another wave of dizziness and fevered chill sweeping over him. It was a long ten minutes before he could get control of himself again, and then only enough to stagger over to the creek and sink down upstream from the body and wash himself. He drank deeply as if unable to get enough, the refreshing water seeming to evaporate before it could reach the back of his throat.

Then he rested, determining what to do next. He didn't know where he was, but it stood to reason that the creek would be travelling toward the San Juan River, and eventually he'd reach the river if he followed its course. And, just as importantly, he'd always be next to the water he now needed so desperately.

Feeling better, he checked over the camp and threw the other weapons away, after loading himself with his Winchester and spare cartridges for it and the pistol. He steeled himself to take the monkey carcass along, for food was food and at this point he couldn't be particular. Then, with a machete to help him slash his way through the thick growth beside the stream, he set off into the dim alien jungle once again. . . .

Hours, days, minutes all merged into one; time became confusion for Kane. It was all he could do to keep placing one foot in front of the other and whack away at the green plants in his way. He had the strange sensation of floating, sounds and colours swirling about him in weird, nonsensical patterns. Night descended and he forced himself to continue through the blackness, stumbling and falling, sometimes on the verge of fainting, using the fresh scent and noise of the water to keep him on course, like a carrot in front of a donkey. His stomach tightened into convulsive knots, refusing even the idea of nourishment. Somewhere along the way, he threw the monkey away into the brush. Somewhere else, he dropped to his knees and fell asleep. By dawn he was moving again, his senses more ethereal and fevered than ever.

When the sun was at its zenith, and Kane entered a small lagoon, he was certain that the image before his eyes was a mirage. A distorted figment of his sick imagination. The figure was of a muscular, tall man, bronzed and naked, fishing in the miniature lake. Kane shook his head, trying to clear his mind. The man refused to disappear, but came closer, smiling, as one might smile at a strange wild animal, tentatively and almost reluctantly. Kane stopped, a wild thought entering his numb mind that indeed he must look like a wild animal to anybody meeting him now.

He held out an empty hand. "A-amigo," he gasped.

The native came over, his touch firm on Kane's shoulder, and now Kane was convinced he wasn't hallucinating. Kane asked: "You . . . speak Spanish?"

"A little," came the guarded reply.

"I need help."

"Si, I help. You give me gift, I help."

Kane tried to give the machete to the Indian, but

discovered the machete was gone. He'd evidently dropped it somewhere, sometime, and hadn't even been aware of it being gone. He thrust the carbine into the outstretched hands instead, knowing he was risking his life. The native could shoot him now as his "help", then rob his corpse at will.

Instead the Indian put the carbine on one shoulder and grasped Kane with his other arm, half-dragging Kane across the water to the opposite shore. "Village near," the Indian said. Kane didn't reply, letting himself be guided as if sleepwalking.

The rest was even more unclear than his trek along the creek. He remembered a whirling vision of huts, fires, naked children, the gagging bitter taste of some liquid that was forced down his throat by a wrinkled old man. . . . It was only later that he learned he'd been delirious for two days and doctored at regular intervals. It was another three days before he'd collected strength enough to totter around the small village while he recovered from his fever, eating and drinking vast quantities and never once bothering to ask what he was consuming. He was sure he wouldn't want to know. The sour medicine, however, he figured was the local equivalent of quinine, and like many native remedies, better than the product of white man's laboratories after centuries of testing.

The wrinkled old man turned out to be two wrinkled old men, each as wizened and as ugly as each other. One was the village Chief, who spoke Spanish quite well and dressed in the filthy remnants of a tropical white suit. As a badge of his office, he always wore a pith helmet, bird plumes stuck into the bands. The second old man was the village witch-doctor, a sort of combination priest and sorcerer who supposedly could lay on spells as well as exorcise them. It was his opinion that Kane had been cursed. Kane wasn't going to argue, not after having had the medicine cure him.

The carbine proved to be Kane's welcome mat. It became village property, each native man getting his turn at pot-shotting for game. When Kane felt well enough, the Chief declared that the carbine's trophies of monkey and boar would serve as an excuse for a village feast. The feast lasted well into the night, becoming wilder and more wanton as it progressed. Kane kept to one side, not wishing to involve himself in the abandoned eating, drinking, and dancing. He didn't feel strong enough; and he'd heard stories about travellers who'd let themselves go, only to discover the next day that local customs demanded that they marry some fat toothless woman because they'd chucked her under the chin or suchlike.

One part of the feast seemed remarkable to Kane, and when he asked the Chief about it, he learned it was a standard item to every celebration. It was a gruesome totem of an alligator, around which the men danced and sung and waved their machetes. Kane was reminded of some of the American Indian gatherings, and the Chief explained that indeed, there was a link to the spirit world in the ugly alligator image. It represented the giant devil beast that was living in the river, eating lots of the fish and animals the villagers would otherwise capture.

"We're fighting the old demon in dance now, because we'll soon select the bravest of us to fight it in real life."

"I see," Kane said. "A pre-fight inspirational."

The Chief shook his head sadly. "So far, the old

demon has eaten every challenger. It has a bad spirit, but a powerful one."

Kane studied the crude statue fashioned of bark and twigs, and painted in wild primitive strokes to indicate the beast. He was more concerned about getting back to the canal project than becoming involved in an alligator hunt. Then like a lightning stroke, a thought occurred to him: the Chief had said *river*! "Tell me," he said then, "this monster can't be living in the creek I was following, could it?"

"It would be seen like a giant rock if it were."

"Then this river it lives in. . . . Where is it?"

"Not far," the Chief answered. "A place that's wide, with sand and mud." He staggered away in search of more pinga.

Kane followed, excited now. This "river" had to be the San Juan! "Chief, listen to me."

The Chief belched, peering bleary-eyed at Kane.

"I am not the bravest among you," Kane said diplomatically, "but I owe your people my life. Let me repay you by being the next challenger of your old demon."

"You're *loco*!"

"Let me take my gun that I gave you and shoot the alligator devil. Your men, brave warriors that they are, may not be as practised with the gun as I am. I promise to return the gun."

Kane watched the Chief mull over his suggestion, frowning and belching again, then glancing over at the old witch-doctor who was leading the ritual dance around the totem. The Chief's eyes narrowed, and Kane wondered if he hated and feared the witch-doctor like so many other tribal Chiefs did. Good witch-doctors were a threat to their power. The old bull 'gator, Kane thought, had probably chewed up a fisherman or two, and from that a legend had been spawned, likely with the enthusiastic help of the doctor, glad to whip up a few routines to protect the native fighters. If Kane, an outsider, could kill the animal, the Chief's authority would be strengthened, and if not, nothing would be lost except Kane.

"Show me the river," Kane urged. "I'll stop your 'gator."

"You do," the Chief said, smiling, "and you are a brother." Then he let out a tremendous, blood-curdling scream. "Hiiah!"

The dance froze in its tracks, the natives stopping to stare. The Chief, all eyes upon him, grinned and pointed to Kane. "White man dare the old demon," he announced. "No more feast, no more dance. We go to river now and he prove he one of us!"

9

The native guide turned and pointed across the inky stretch of river, his finger shaking. In the weak starlight, Kane couldn't tell what exactly the Indian was gesturing toward, but he supposed by the vague curve of the San Juan that it was at the flat, muddy crescent across the bank from them. It was a cratered area where silt and rock and torn-up trees had collected during floods, but it was barren of life, the trees only gnarled logs and the earth desolate ooze.

"What's over there that makes you fight over it?" Kane asked.

"Fish," the Indian answered. "There are small

pools and eddies where insects grow, and where insects grow, fish grow."

"And the old demon?"

"It eats the fish, our fish, and the small animals that come to forage there too. It eats us, if we come." The native was shaking like a leaf now. "It's huge, white man, like one of those big trees. Like a dart from a blow-gun, it is quick."

"Big and fast," Kane murmured, reached down beside him in the canoe and bringing up the Winchester. "But not as fast as a bullet from this, amigo, or as big as what it can do."

The native rolled his eyes, uncertain of anything, and rowed faster across the quiet, brackish water. Big and fast and undoubtedly smart, Kane thought; he'd heard of similar shrewd 'gators in the Florida swamps, but down here they were supposed to grow fatter and meaner than anywhere else. Still, a 'gator is only an animal. These natives living inland obviously didn't know that much about them to be putting so much store in this particular brute. But then, *he* didn't know much about 'gators, either.

They reached the opposite shore, at the lip of the long curve. Gingerly, Kane eased himself out of the canoe, standing unsteadily in the mire. "You wait here for me, savvy?"

The native nodded his head. He'd been the warrior the witch-doctor had chosen to fight the old demon tonight, so he was quite prepared to sit this one out while Kane did his deed. "You should've had yourself made invunerable," he said.

Kane smiled sardonically in the darkness, thinking of the evil-smelling concoction the witch-doctor had brewed. He'd turned down the chance of having it spread on his body, and in doing so had further angered the Doc. No doubt curses were being muttered against him right now, Kane figured; this was as much a contest between the Doc and the Chief as it was between him and this fabled 'gator.

He shook his thoughts off and concentrated on stalking the beast. He moved deeper across the wide, marshy spit, sinking into puddles and gumbo, tripping over invisible roots and stray branches. The peninsula was pockmarked with black holes and burrowing caves, any one of them suitable for the 'gator to nest in. What made Kane curious about this hunt, was the fact that all the natives agreed that their old demon *came down to the water*, whereas most 'gators he'd ever heard about lived in the banks, not up on dry land. It made him think of some gruesome prehistoric reptile, unseen and unchanged for millions of years, lurking in the dank mud.

Now he was scaring himself! Kane gritted his teeth, telling himself forcefully that he was out after nothing but a strong bull 'gator a little bit bigger and nastier than usual.

Deeper across the stretch he went, among the tree stumps and boulders. Up close, the flatness disappeared and became ridges and crests like mesas in the Arizona badlands. It was a sterile land of fantastic bridges and gateways between muddy holes, and when Kane sat down on one of the tree roots, he realised he'd been the noisiest thing there. Everything else was silent.

Kane sat for a long time, waiting. He could spend the entire night thrashing around among the shadows and black pits, and never once catch sight or sound of the 'gator. He was in a good position where he was, centrally located and quite high up. He could even see across the river now, toward the opposite bank where the Chief and his tribe were also waiting, and he judged that to be a good quarter-mile away. So he was best off staying put for awhile, and see if anything developed.

While he waited, it occurred to Kane that he'd passed this spit on his trip upriver to the canal. It had looked entirely different in the daylight, of course, and the perspective was turned all around from there, but this eroded plateau was the only one of its kind he'd seen, and he'd been struck by its presence at the time. It'd been a day away from the canal project, which meant he was now quite farther from his goal than he'd first estimated. The thought made him despondent, and he almost didn't see the slight blending of shadows on his right.

The movement was so silent and swift that Kane wasn't sure it had taken place, even as he swivelled to face it. He peered into the gloom, wondering if his imagination was playing tricks on him or if it'd been a tiny frog or some other harmless creature or. . . . He shuddered responsively, gripping the carbine tighter.

Nothing more. Slowly Kane turned away again. Then in the corner of his eye, he saw it happen a second time, and now he was positive. Something low and black was gliding among the trees and boulders, something as agile as a snake yet very large. . . . It was all Kane could do to stay put and not run like blazes for the canoe. But damn its eyes, no stinking old 'gator was going to make him retreat—especially not in front of the tribe and that cynical witch-doctor! Pride rooted him to his position.

The shadows seemed to close in on Kane, the *lack* of noise more frightening than if there'd been some godalmighty roar. Kane kept his finger stiff on the trigger of his carbine, aiming it in the general direction of the shifting darkness, thinking all the while the 'gator could be sneaking up behind him. A scrape of a root to his left now; Kane jerked, trying to get a lead on whatever had caused the tiny sound. Again nothing. Then like abruptly lit lanterns, two glowing eyes appeared out of nowhere.

"Sonofabitch!" Kane shouted as the shadows reared up. It *was* a monster, he thought in that split instant; a giant of a nightmare, all teeth and claws and scaley hide. Two phosphorescent eyes, one pink cave of a mouth, row upon row of white fangs, and the rest the colour of midnight in a coal mine! It *hissed* at him like steam escaping from a locomotive, and came at him like one, so fast and so near that the carbine couldn't be brought to bear in time. Kane scrambled backward over the tree root, losing his footing and almost falling, grabbing for his Colt revolver to blast away at close quarters.

The shadows parted, and now Kane realised that there was more than just a huge alligator attacking him. Other things, hairy and clawing, were lunging from the sidelines. Kane peppered shots as fast as he could, seeing one of the hairy things fold up and drop away from the tree. Then the night was blotted out as the alligator—or whatever the old demon was—landed on him. He jerked his arm straight up in a panicky uppercut that saved his face from being mauled, firing into the tough abdomen of the creature at the same time. More hisses, and the stink of warm blood rivuleted over his clothes. Then there was an agonizing pain that seared up from his thigh to his brain as the beast tore into his leg with its claws.

Kane twisted and writhed in frantic desperation, firing his fifth shot. The alligator devil shuddered, sliding to one side and allowed Kane to wriggle free. But Kane knew there was still plenty of fight in whatever it was, and that he only had one bullet left. Pride was one thing—this was damn foolishness to stick around for the finish! He vaulted from the log and hobbled with every last bit of energy in a very rapid retreat to the canoe. The pain from his wound was setting fire to his insides, and he knew he had only moments before he'd black out.

Ahead of him there was a high-pitched scream. The native guide dove overboard and was swimming for all his might across the river, not even waiting for Kane to help paddle the canoe in his hysterical flight. The old demon was still coming after Kane, but the sound of the scream and the splash of water distracted it. It veered diagonally, angling for the water and the native. Kane fired his last shot in an attempt to dissuade the beast, but it was useless. The water rippled and bubbled and then there was only the noise of the swimmer.

Kane dropped into the canoe, reaching for the paddle and surged out across the river to intercept the native. But this effort was too great. The torture in his leg overwhelmed him, and he fell back uncontrollably, the paddle falling into the water. Unconsciousness stole over him, blanking out the fetid water at the bottom of the canoe, and the strangling cries of the native being eaten alive. . . .

Gwen Arling frowned as she peered across the expanse of daylit river. She leaned forward and tapped the nearest native on the shoulder. He turned, pausing in midstroke with his paddle, upsetting the rhythm the other two natives were maintaining.

"Si, señorita?"

"That's a canoe drifting toward us, isn't it?" She was pointing now toward a distant floating object, bobbing and weaving in the gentle current. In the shimmering light that seeped through the overhanging vines and tree branches, the object kept changing from a canoe to a log then back to a canoe. But as it neared them, its outline was becoming more distinct.

"Si, señorita," the Indian confirmed.

"An empty canoe. . . ." Gwen frowned, knowing how important canoes were to the tribes along the river; how the loss of one would be great, and what care they took not to have one drift free. The Indian was shaking his head, however, and said in broken Spanish: "Not empty, señorita, it ride too low."

"Row over to it," she ordered.

The three natives who'd accompanied her from Colon dug in with their paddles, braving a cross-current to angle toward the canoe. The leader grasped hold of the bark side, sucked in his breath, and stared.

"What's wrong?" Gwen asked, rising up to look. She saw a muddy boot, and then a bloody, encrusted hand. "A man—"

"A dead man, señorita. We'd best let him ride his own way."

Gwen ignored the spiritual advice, craning still further until she could see Morgan Kane's ragged, bearded features. "Oh my God," she whispered in horror, then to the natives: "Row, row like never before, to the bank."

The natives leaned into the oars while Gwen held onto Kane's canoe and towed it along with them. Up on shore, they lifted Kane from his canoe and carried him to a soft, mossy patch. Gwen knelt and checked for a pulse, afraid the natives were right and Kane was dead. No—there was a feeble pulse! There was still a chance. . . . "My bag, quickly, get it from the canoe," she ordered. "And blankets. Yes, and light a fire and boil some water, too. This man's very sick, but he's still alive."

The Indians sprang to her command. The doctor had been disappointed about much of the canal project she'd seen in Panama but the clever and conscientious natives had impressed her tremendously. These three especially appealed to her, and in turn they obeyed her strange foreign orders with blind loyal obedience. Within half an hour, Kane was wrapped naked in the blankets, his jaw clenched and his teeth chattered slightly.

She raised an eyelid and looked at the dull pupil. "Malaria," she muttered to herself, rising to fetch quinine for him. It was worse then just the fever itself, for there was an ugly gash along his thigh, puffed with infection. She believed she'd be able to stop it from spreading by disinfecting and bandaging the wound after the natives had washed him thoroughly. But there was a great loss of blood, adding to his weakened condition, and perhaps overloading his palpitating heart.

Only time could tell.

She forced the quinine between his compressed lips. He tried to shake himself free, even though unconscious, thrashing and moaning, one phrase being repeated over and over: *the old demon.*

Old demon? It made no sense to Gwen, only heightening her curiosity as to what had happened to Kane. And while inspecting his wound, she couldn't help but note how the rest of his lean, wire-taut body was covered with scars and marks—the symbols of his brutal way of life. Even now, as Kane eased slowly into a more gentle slumber, his face did not lose its ravaged, almost cruel appearance. There was nothing soft in him, nothing warm, not even deep inside that might surface when he was asleep or unconscious.

It seemed ironic to Gwen Arling, that she was saving this man's life. His features were the living testimony to the validity of her shipboard comments. And yet, she had to admit they were also the confirmation of her secret attraction for him. . . .

Around midnight, she was tending the fire by herself. Her three natives were asleep nearby, and Kane had not yet regained his senses. Suddenly he began to become feverish again, groaning and waving his arms, chanting "old demon, old demon" through his teeth. She held him, trying to calm and warm his shivering body. He clutched her as a child might its mother, totally unaware of what he was doing. She let him, staring up at the night sky with amusement. She thought of her teacher at the medical university, and how he'd probably have approved of her method for treating her patient. She felt a little noble doing it, as if somehow their embrace was a personal sacrifice . . . but there was a devil down inside her, saying that it was enjoyable too, and she felt a bit irresponsible and attracted by her own lack of propriety. It was the woman in her fighting with the doctor, and she couldn't help wondering which force would win if Kane suddenly woke up. . . .

The night slowly evolved into early dawn. The San Juan River flowed on its soundless course to the sea through the twists of jungle growth. Kane, the girl, and the three Indians were the only ones there. The Indian tribe who'd shown Kane to the river had long since returned to their village, convinced the old demon had eaten another villager and the white man too.

10

When Morgan Kane first became conscious, he was convinced Dr Gwen Arling was an hallucination. But she soon proved she wasn't a product of his fever, as she tended him with efficient care, smiling all the while with an almost wistful expression. Kane had no way of knowing why the fact he was helpless was a strong attraction for her, countering her previous image of him as nothing but a heartless, conscienceless machine of destruction. But he could tell she was nursing him with more personal attention than was needed, and that she was showing affection as well as doctoring skill.

He tried to throw off her growing appeal. But he was too weak to keep up the emotional barriers, and fight the temptations she offered. It was all he could do just to regain his physical strength, and force himself to hobble around on his wounded leg. It hurt like hell, his leg, but he knew he had to keep exercising it if it was not to become stiff and cramped, with possibly a permanent injury.

The three natives with Gwen kept the camp and fire going while she tended to Kane, and Kane gradually healed. Days passed, mostly in silence, with Kane reluctant to talk about how he'd wound up in the canoe more dead than alive. Gwen told him that her canoe was filled with medicine for the Nicaraguan project, and Kane recalled that the young doctor there had considered calling on the French in Panama to help restock his dwindling supplies. The Panama canal itself was progressing slowly but surely, she reported, and sickness had decreased sufficiently so that Dr Schwartz and the two aides could get along without her for awhile. She asked him if his wound had come from a knife; Kane refused to confirm or deny, but changed the subject instead. She tried to draw him into conversation a few times after that, but soon she learned he wouldn't be pressed. He'd tell her when and if he was ready, and not before.

The last day together in the camp, Kane sat absorbed in thought all morning. Gwen talked of nothing but leaving today, Kane being well enough now to travel, and Kane realised he'd have to tell her something in order to postpone the journey. He didn't know where to begin, or how much to relate. He vacillated, exercising his still troublesome leg and checking his revolver. The Indians had machetes, and Gwen carried a nickel-plated .32 pistol on her hip, but that was all. No rifles. It had been out of luck, not design, that his revolver had ended up in the bottom of the canoe along with him, for those last few minutes back on the marshy flat had been too insane for any rational thoughts. Carefully he cleaned his revolver, as he had on preceding days, inspecting his remaining cartridges for signs of rust.

Finally, when he couldn't put off telling Gwen any longer, he called her over to one side, sat her down, and haltingly recounted his adventures. He told of the snipers, the jungle trek to smoke them out, the fight and how he'd been taken prisoner. Then how he'd escaped, stumbled downstream to a friendly tribe, which had then led him to the San Juan. He left out nothing, not even about finding the Hotchkiss rifles, except for one fact: the old demon. Kane completely avoided any mention of his hunt for the devil 'gator across the wide mud spit with its jumble of trees and boulders. He didn't tell her because Kane wasn't sure what the truth was—what he'd found in the darkness; what exactly he'd seen and felt and shot. Only the fact that his gun was empty convinced him he hadn't dreamed the entire nightmare during one of his feverish periods.

And, wisely, Gwen didn't ask, knowing that it would be useless and Kane would resent her prying. But she also knew he was leading up to something now, and she said: "You want something, Morgan?"

Kane nodded. "Yes. I want you to stay here one more night."

"And you?"

"I . . . I'll be taking my canoe upriver again. But I'll be back tomorrow morning, and then we can push on for the canal."

"But why?"

Kane glared down at his boots, not answering.

Gwen pursed her lips. "Well, I'll be coming with you."

"No."

"Don't be silly. You can't go in your condition."

"I must. And you must *not*."

"Morgan, you're acting childish. It's as if . . . as if you're on some sort of personal crusade you can't even dare to whisper to me, like a little boy with a secret."

Kane straightened, frowning at her, his voice

biting. "Then I'm being a child, Gwen. But I'm not doing it like a vendetta of my own, you've got to believe me. I'm doing it because I have to, because there's. . . . There's *something* upriver that's in our way."

"What?"

"I don't know, don't you see?"

"Is it an old demon?"

Kane turned pale, clenching his teeth. "Call it whatever you fancy. But it's got to be stopped, and I'm the only one around here who's got any chance of stopping it."

Dr Arling was suddenly aware that Kane was frightened. It almost frightened her, seeing him this way, his eyes black with torment. She realised it was taking every bit of stamina he possessed to force himself into facing this *something* upriver.

"If I don't come back tomorrow," Kane continued, "have the Indians paddle upriver on this side only. Is that clear?"

She nodded, not knowing what to say now.

Kane looked at her a long while. Then, smiling almost sadly, he turned and started down the bank to his canoe. The Indians, not knowing why he was leaving, laughed and waved to him as he paddled out into the river. He hefted his oar in a salute, and within a few moments had disappeared among the low lying trees. . . .

Night sounds enveloped the camp, but to Gwen, it was empty now without Kane near her. She tossed more wood on the fire, feeling cold and clammy—not from any fever, but from a sensation of weird horror and apprehension. The rough, soulless man had proven to her he was weak at times and awkward at others, all without realizing it. He'd shown himself to be *human*—and like the descriptions of American Indians, something of a noble savage. And he was out there alone someplace, up against something he called an "old demon", and of which he was obviously frightened.

Her thoughts moved on to what he'd told her about finding French-made rifles in the hands of the snipers. Kane hadn't given any conclusions, but the inference was clear—that de Lessup's canal company was behind the sabotage and killings. The idea made her dizzy with horror—it just couldn't be true! If it were, it not only involved the French, but the Colombian government as well, since all weapon shipments went through their hands. Was the entire operation completely corrupt and ruthless?

Gwen was so involved in her own thoughts, that she was unaware when her Indians rose and went to the edge of the river. Then one called to her, and jerking upwards, she heard him say: "Señorita, a canoe comes!"

Kane! was her first thought as she ran to where the natives were standing. But now she saw that out of the darkness, the canoe was much larger than Kane's, and was filled with three Jamaicans and two white men. "Hello on shore!" a white man called out.

"Hello!" she called back tentatively, the same chill as before coursing up her spine. The canoe touched shore, and the men came up on the bank beside her. The Jamaicans were heavily armed with rifles, knives and revolvers. The two white men she recognised as being Kanter and Streicher, the security chief and his body guard from Colon, even though they were now wearing grubby clothes instead of fine linen suits.

"Dr Arling, I'll be—ah, darned," Kanter said, smiling. "We heard you were on your way to the Nicaraguan project, but we never expected to run across you out here now."

"We were delayed," she said, unable to stifle the odd nervousness which was creeping over her. "But what are you doing here?"

"Business," Kanter said, and made a shrugging gesture. "We've heard there are more workers available than are needed here."

"I haven't heard that."

"It could well be a false lead, Dr Arling, but it's worth checking on. We need all the hands we can get down in Panama."

Streicher spoke now for the first time, his eyes narrow and his voice thin with suspicion. "Are you alright, Doc?"

"Why, of course I am. Why do you ask?"

"You said you were delayed. Your natives look well, and your canoe seems fine, so I was wondering. . . . Worried, y'know."

"No, we were held up because of Mr Kane."

"Kane!" Kanter burst out. "Morgan Kane?"

"Why, yes. We found him in a canoe, wounded and drifting downriver."

"Where is he, Doctor?"

Gwen shrunk back from his sharp tone. "Why, why I'm not sure. He took his canoe and went back upriver to look for something."

"Look for what?"

"He wouldn't say, just . . . just *something*."

"How was he wounded, did he say?"

"Not exactly, but I gather it was from when he was taken prisoner and escaped. But really, Mr Kanter, I don't understand—"

"Did he say who'd taken him prisoner?"

"No. These bands of terrorists, I assume." She looked at both men quizzically, then added crossly: "I don't care for your questioning at all, Mr Kanter. There's no call to be rude."

"Please, excuse me." Kanter's toady face softened into a placating smile. "I didn't mean to offend you. It's just that . . . well, as Mr Streicher here has said, we're worried about Mr Kane. He's very new to these parts, you know, and has obviously fallen into a bad situation. We want to help if at all possible. Are you *sure* he didn't tell you where he was going or why?"

"I'm quite positive, and—"

"Hoi!" The barking interruption came from one of the Jamaicans, who had been standing beside a native of Gwen's. "Listen, *patron,* listen to what this hombre say."

The native Indian was shaking his head, eyes wide.

The Jamaican grabbed hold of the man's arm and twisted it viciously. Dr Arling stepped forward. "Let him go this instant!"

"Si, Bobo," Kanter added with a nod. He went to the native and glared into the eyes. "What were you saying, eh?"

The native still refused to talk, more out of fear than defiance. Bobo, the Jamaican, grimaced and said: "He say 'demon'."

"Demon!" Streicher snarled. Kanter turned to face Dr Arling, his face gnarled with his emotion. "It that true? Is Kane after the old demon?"

"He. . . ."

"Is he?"

"I tell you, I don't know! Mr Kane raved about a

demon while he was delirious with fever. That's what was overheard, not his destination—that he wouldn't tell me other than it was upriver."

"Upriver," Streicher said, clutching Kanter's shoulder. "It has to be the old demon, it's the only answer."

"You're right, Franz. We'll leave immediately. And Dr Arling, we'll be taking your canoe as well."

"I beg your pardon! You'll do no such—"

"There's no time to lose! We may need a spare, and it'll give us a better chance against *it*. Don't argue, in this instance I know better than you, than any of you here." Kanter turned away, barking orders to the other Jamaicans. Streicher moved swiftly to Gwen's canoe and climbed into it with Bobo.

Gwen, angered, stepped up to Kanter and faced him. "I don't believe you do know better, Mr Kanter. After all, I am a doctor and I am quite conversed in the rantings of fevered patients."

"But you are not educated in the ways of the jungle, young lady," Kanter snapped back. "I know better because I know this area, and I know that Mr Kane was not merely dreaming wildly. I know because *I have seen the old demon with my own eyes!*"

11

The muddy tongue lay dark and menacing under the starlight. Kane glided his canoe soundlessly through the river water until it gently nudged two sprawling roots. He waded ashore, dragging the canoe with him and stashed it between the roots, then moved higher along the soggy ground, machete and revolver held ready.

After a short time of searching, he found the place where he'd battled the old demon. It had to be a huge bull 'gator, he told himself; it had to be an optical illusion that had made it seem as if it'd risen right out of the ground. The eyes flashing had been only a reflection of starlight in a reptile's face, that was all! It *had* to be that, and nothing more. . . . Kane, determined to settle the issue one way or another—to see the beast in hell if need be—crept slowly around, seeking the 'gator's lair. The stench of the mud was thick, cloying to his nostrils. The ground was slippery, his boots leaving oozing indentations that filled with brackish water behind him. No sign of the old demon, or of the weird hairy shapes that had attacked him from the sides.

A noise!

Kane paused in mid-step, craning around to hear. Only dimly could he see the trees and rocks, their separate outlines blurring into a single phalanx of greys and blacks. Yet one figure seemed a little too round, a little too smooth for a rock or tree trunk. Kane focused on it, hesitating. . . . The thing moved.

Old demon!

Kane dragged his wounded, stiff thigh up under himself, and crouched where he was, poised for an attack. Now he could see that the shadow was moving to the right, slowly and in awkward jerks, as an alligator moves when on shore. Suddenly it became shorter and thicker, and Kane realised that the reptile had now turned to face him, so that he saw it front-on. The shadow stayed motionless for a long time. Kane moved gradually aside, avoiding a root he might've sprawled over during a fight. His leg sunk into the mucky gumbo, and when he pulled free, the suction made a soft slurping sound. Again Kane froze, fearful that the 'gator had heard the noise. He gripped the handle of his revolver, seeing the shadows slowly respond. He clicked back the pistol's hammer with the palm of his left hand, muffling the slight noise. The creature was too far away and still too indistinct to waste bullets on, but it was coming closer . . . and Kane was now moving toward it as well. He kept low, angling in a hunched crawl so that he wouldn't be silhouetted against the silvery band of the river at back of him.

The shadow stopped, as if pausing with indecision. It lay still, blended back into the mud, vanishing from Kane's view even as he was peering toward it. Another sound—Kane swivelled to face it—then another—Kane turned back seeing the great black object looming up over the mudbanks, low and swift. Kane raised his revolver, sighting with outstretched arms, and with a mingling of rage, fear, and satisfaction, waited till the *something* was right in line.

And then he fired.

A wailing cry rose up, echoing across the peninsula, and the thing fell back into the blackness. Kane moved forward, re-cocking and bringing his pistol up to aim again. The shadow remained motionless. He reached and stared down at the huddled mass, then with a snarl, swivelled about and began clambering over the rocks and trees, in search of other old demons. The pain in his leg was acute; he tried to ignore it, but sharp lightning bolts seared up with every move he made, making him wince and falter. The darkness lengthened, and Kane now realised he was in a larger hollow than he'd first imagined, and that the pitch black depths around him stretched away until he couldn't see their limits.

A whisper beside him! Something else moved, and Kane barely caught its flickering motion to his side. He threw himself to the other side, sighting on two luminous eyes and a hissing pink mouth. Kane blasted with his gun just as a scaly, clawed foot slashed through the night and hit him on the head with violent strength. Dazed, Kane stumbled backwards, slipping in the mud and hitting his head against a wall behind him. He wasn't conscious of firing his pistol all this while—five, sharp shots pumping into the old demon, making it writhe and hiss and then groan convulsively. Simultaneously, Kane and the creature tumbled into the ooze, blanking into unconsciousness.

"Turn in here," Kanter ordered.

The two negro Jamaicans manoeuvred their canoe against the muddy bank of the peninsula. Then the other canoe, with Streicher, Bobo, and Gwen Arling, touched shore beside him. Once aground, they moved forward, Kanter and Streicher in determined crouches, the Jamaicans with trepidation, and Dr Arling with nausea from the overwhelming stench rising from the fetid area.

Then came a pistol shot. All of them stopped short; startled, wary about going on. Streicher said after a long moment: "Do you think we should—" and then his thought was cut off by the sound of more shots, a series of them resounding across the marshy flatland. Finally, silence.

Again they hesitated. The silence stretched on endlessly, until Kanter couldn't stand the suspense and indecision any longer. "We've got to do something, Franz."

Streicher nodded. "It could mean Matt."

"Matt?" Gwen looked puzzled. "You mean Mr Kane."

Kanter glanced at the lady doctor, nervously wiping his hands on his pants. "Mr Kane? Why yes of course, m' dear." Then to Kanter, he said harshly: "Let's get moving."

They stumbled upwards along the bank, deeper into the brackish mire, staggering and sliding in their haste. Gwen struggled to keep pace, her mind whirling with confusion, fear for Morgan Kane, and horror of the horrid, evil place they'd landed. She couldn't understand a bit of what had been going on, the surprising visit by Kanter and Streicher only adding to a mystery Kane had begun for her. Then to be shuttled unceremoniously into her own canoe, whipped away on some urgent and obviously perilous mission while her natives were left to guard the medicine. . . . It was all too much for her to accept. And this place was absolutely loathesome!

There came a sharp cry from Streicher, and Kanter went to where he was standing. Gwen couldn't see clearly from where she was; it seemed to her that they were inspecting a large shaggy fur rug that was lying in a bundled-up heap on the soil.

"Dead," Streicher said. "God *damn* it."

"Matt!" Kanter called, running again across the rock and tree-strewn peninsula. "Matt!"

Gwen backed away from the spot where the fur rug was lying unable to bring herself to take a closer look. Instinctively, she knew she didn't want to find out what it was.

"*Matt!*"

Still they surged on, Gwen gasping for breath, and the two white men a few yards ahead of her, oblivious to anything except this mysterious "Matt" they were calling. For a weird instant, Gwen imagined somehow that they were meaning "mat," and it was in connection with the "rug" on the ground, then her nonsensical thoughts vanished as she heard a low, muffled voice answer from the inky well of a nearby mound of boulders.

"Heerrree . . ." it moaned throatily.

Kanter gave out a bark of laughter. "Are you okay, Matt?"

"Yes. Come on."

Gwen had finally caught up to the men now, and clutched at Streicher's sleeve before they could go to the voice. "Wait. . . . Wait a minute, please. . . ."

"No time," he said sharply, then called: "Matt, did you get the snooping Kane?"

"I don't know no names, but there's a man here dead," answered the grumbling voice. "Come on closer, *patron*. . . ."

"Morgan!" Gwen choked, and felt herself dizzy, as if ready to faint. Streicher clutched her, forcing her upright. "Keep on your feet, lady," he snapped. "And come on!"

She was nearly yanked off her feet by Streicher's tug, and it was all she could do to keep her balance as he shoved her along with him. She recalled her small pistol and groped for it now, but felt the empty holster on her hip. A sinking sensation rippled through her. There was no question now in her mind: Kane was dead, and these two men were in on his killing! They'd even disarmed her, Streicher picking her holster sometime while they were on the way here in the canoe! A small helpless whimper escaped from her lips, but Streicher ignored her torment, dragging her brutally through the mud and slime toward the boulders.

The Jamaican negroes were on either side of them, keeping even with them as they approached. Gwen knew the taste of defeat, aware there would be no escape for her now. She couldn't outrun the negroes even if she could elude Kanter and Streicher, and she couldn't defend herself either. This "Matt" person was the most important thing on their minds right now, but sooner or later they'd get around to disposing of her, just like they'd taken care of Morgan Kane. Her tomb would be this ghastly mud flat.

"Where are you?" Kanter asked in a loud voice, the boulders straight ahead of them. "C'mon, Matt, show yourself!"

"All right."

In the weak light, Gwen Arling saw a terrible monster rise up from the black pit of the rocks. It was an alligator so huge that she cried out with involuntary shock as well as fright. Phosphorescent eyes glittered coldly at her, and then the great beast grew even more enormous, standing upon its hind legs and swaying over them. Its long snout opened, displaying rows of sharp fangs. Gwen thought she was going to go mad. This was *Matt*?

Then the erect, monstrous alligator did something which made her scream shrilly in the night. It slowly began to shed its hide. The scaly flesh split in two and fell away, just as Kanter was again barking with his cold laughter. "Christ, Matt! You were even scaring me a li'le, coming out like that. Now—"

"Watch out! It's Kane!" Streicher yelled suddenly.

The skin sloughing off around his form, the unmistakable features of Kane could now be seen. His face was contorted with rage and hatred, and in his hand was his revolver. Streicher was moving like the snake he was, whipping up his hammerless "banker's special" pistol from inside his jacket. But fast as he was, he couldn't outdraw an already levelled gun.

Kane stood with the alligator hide pooled around his legs and blasted Streicher with swift efficiency. Gwen jerked away from Streicher as he crumpled beside her, hearing herself scream again as she stared down at his headless neck squirting blood out in pulsating red jets. Her shrieks mingled with the staccato sounds of more gunsmoke reckonings. Kanter clutched his midriff, hinging in half and dropping his revolver, dying before he hit the mud. Kane angled around, fanning to hit the deadly Jamaicans who were training rifles and revolvers on him, not even flinching when a bullet ricochetted off the stone wall behind him and bit into his face with stinging shards. Two Jamaicans cried and yelled, jerking like puppets on a string, then fell to lie thrashing in the bloody muck.

The fight lasted only seconds. But to Gwen it seemed like an eternity, and for Kanter, Streicher, and their henchmen, it was. Slowly the sounds drifted away, to be swallowed by the jungle. She shivered, trying to stay upright, barely aware of the peculiar limping sound approaching and the firm arm that was drawing her to a warm, heavily beating chest. She placed her hands against the sweat-soaked front of Kane's shirt, looked up into his face for a moment, and then pressed herself tighter. She let herself go, crying in convulsive sobs from relief and from the horror, her cool, professional exterior finally punctured, leaving her exposed, her complacency forever shattered. . . .

Some moments passed before Kane thought she was capable of continuing. Gently he asked her: "Do you have a match?"

"Y-yes."

Gwen fumbled in her pockets, and handed over a wax-paper-wrapped wad of sulphur matches. Kane lit one, shielding it so that the light fell away from the boulders and toward the wall his back had been against. Gwen bit the skin of her hand to keep from screaming yet again, seeing the body of the largest man she'd ever imagined, lying on the ground. He was a mulatto, his brown muscular torso peppered with gunshot wounds. His eyes were open, staring sightlessly at the alligator hide Kane had been hiding in, and now she saw that the hide was built like a huge coat, stuffed with grass to fill out its form, not even the Herculean-sized mulatto large enough for it.

The match dimmed and went out, leaving them in the dark.

"That's the 'old demon'," Kane said savagely. "That's Matt."

"You mean he . . . he dressed up in that thing?"

Kane nodded, gritting his teeth. Gwen frowned, glancing down at his leg, then back up into his pain-flecked eyes. "You're hurt!" she gasped. "God, lie down and let me—"

"No, no, I'll be alright. It's just the leg again. I think the cut opened up again with all these carrying-ons. I'm fine besides that."

"But you—"

"Too much to do, Gwen," Kane interrupted a second time. "Look at that wall behind us, for example. Does it mean anything to you?"

"No, it doesn't. Why?"

"Old fortifications, if I don't miss my guess. This place would've been perfect for the Spaniards to control the river from, and there're more ruins on the other side. I saw some light and heard a few voices further on. And Matt was trying to make it like the olden days, I figure, scaring away the natives and watching the river traffic, and killing anybody who got too curious about the strange action here. Yeah, Matt and another mulatto, dressed up in these weird skins."

"Where did they get them?"

Kane kicked at the costume Matt had been in. "I bet there was an ol' bull 'gator in this swamp, big and mean enough to give the natives second thoughts. Matt or one of them killed it with rifles, then cured the hide—that's the brute they used, painting its eyes with phosphorescent paint, and capitalizing on its reputation to build some bugaboo legends. The other wore a hairy outfit like a bearskin coat, imported from way north, and like nothing ever witnessed in these here parts before."

Kane's voice became hoarse and cruel. A shiver passed through Gwen, even as she clutched him, for she realised that he must have killed all the mulattos involved, like a butcher at a slaughter. To hide her trembling, she asked: "What are we going to do now?"

"Depends on whether you can shoot a gun or not."

"Yes. I'm not a crack shot like you, but I've practised."

"Then here." He gave her a large pistol and watched carefully as she checked over it by the light of a second match. He grunted, reassured by the way she handled it, but it was far too large a weapon for her, and its kick would probably send her flat. "Keep behind me," he told her, "and if there's trouble, you throw yourself down, out of the way."

"Don't worry about that!" she replied fervently.

Kane limped to where the wall had crumbled into ruins, stepping across and continuing on toward the thick trees along the river bank. She could see he was in great pain and was walking poorly, clenching his teeth and holding onto his leg with one hand as if to brace it. She wanted to tell him to give up his search and go back with her to the canoes. In her camp downriver she could bandage him properly, and then maybe—

"Oh!"

He swung around at her startled outburst. "What is it?"

"I . . . I was thinking about the canoes we came in."

"Yes?"

"One of them is mine, the one Streicher and a Jamaican he called Bobo rowed with me. I just remembered that Bobo wasn't among the Jamaicans you . . . shot back there."

"I downed two. You mean Kanter had three along?"

She nodded. "Does that mean he's after us?"

Kane's eyes narrowed, then he shook his head. "No. . . . And it doesn't mean he's afraid of the old demon and has run away. He might've run after hearing the shots, or after seeing his *patrons* go down—or he might be going for help. Damnit!"

"What can we do about him?"

"Nothing now. Nothing at all."

They moved on in the direction Kane had seen a weak light and heard voices. The jungle closed around them, toads croaking in a solemn chorus. Kane strained to see through the gloom to catch sight of the light again or hear those murmuring voices. But except for the toads, the jungle was quiet. The shots or Bobo must've warned whoever was there, he thought grimly, but he pressed on anyway, his only other choice being to return and let Dr Arling patch him up. He didn't want to. He wanted to see this through to the end, even if it meant he was being "childish" as she'd called him earlier.

They brushed through some ferns and clinging vines, passing between a series of tall, thick trees, and coming out on a small knoll overlooking a scrubby clearing. A few ramshackle huts competed with the Spanish ruins and encroaching plants. It wasn't much, but what there was told Kane enough —somebody had been cutting a village out of the midst of the jungle.

"Stay back," he said to Gwen in a low voice. "I'll check."

A voice echoed across the clearing: "Mr Kane? Oh, Kane?"

Kane jerked upright, staring into the jungle at the right side of the clearing. "It's me, Schlesinger," the voice called out, and now Kane could see branches and leaves rustling among the cluster of fallen trees and macheted scrub.

"Schlesinger? What are you doing here?"

"I was going to ask you the same," the engineer said, trooping into view. "I heard some shots up at my camp and thought I'd better investigate, what with all this sabotage going on. What is this crazy place, anyway, and what's going on?"

Kane lowered his pistol, letting his breath out

slowly. "A long story, believe me. But I figure these are part of some ruins left over from the Spanish occupation, and that somebody's been wanting to keep them to himself."

"Sure, that'd explain all the sabotage." Schlesinger stood in the middle of the ruins, shaking his head. Around him three Jamaican labourers were grouped, who were also glancing nervously about. "A centuries-old fort! It'd be a sensational discovery, worth a lot of money. Hey, is that somebody with you?"

"Dr Arling. She's going to help with the clinic at the canal."

"That's great. Come on, Morgan, and bring her too, and tell me what the devil's been going on. All these shots and everything, and you disappearing for days on end. Why, we thought you were dead for sure."

A shiver of apprehension spiralled up Kane's backbone, but he stifled it with a smile. "You heard the shots, did you?"

"Yeah, my camp's about a mile or so further up. We must've been passing close by this for a long time, and never knew it."

"Kanter knew about it."

"What?"

"Only Kanter's dead," Kane said, no longer smiling.

"And you will be too if you move, señor," a cold voice said from behind Kane. "Stand easy, and drop your gun. Pronto!"

Colonel Valparaiso!

Kane lowered his pistol, letting it drop to the ground.

"Gracias," the Colonel said. "And you, señorita, you too. As it is you can barely lift that cannon with your hand. Eh, bueno. Now, go stand over on the right side of Señor Kane. No, the *right* side, that's it. Both of you, remember I've a rifle trained on you, and from this distance, I can't miss."

Kane stared straight ahead, his lips pressed firm with sudden fury. The soft grey false-dawn was outlining more of the clearing now, illuminating the smug expression on the engineer's face. Kane saw more than just Schlesinger; he saw the entire plot, which extended further than to just Kanter and Streicher. The attempt on Colonel Valparaiso's life back in Colon had been merely stage-setting, to lull suspicion and give the Colonel more power in order to "rid the area of terrorist killers." And the engineer had discovered the old fortification long ago, and had entered in on a subtle conspiracy to cash in on his find. What better people to turn to for help than those working for the French—who'd love to foul up the American project and get rich while doing it. It wasn't difficult to deduce Valparaiso's motive: pure greed. Under the jungle scrub would be artifacts and museum treasures, if not gold and silver by the ton. Melted down or sold as antiquities, what lay buried around here amounted to a fortune many times over. Well worth killing for.

"What now Colonel?" he said between his teeth.

"That remains to be seen, Señ—ugh!" Valparaiso's last sound was a soft, startled grunt, and he slapped at his neck with his left hand as if stung by an insect. But his neck hadn't been bitten by any bug. A tiny dart had pierced his flesh, and with horrified eyes he staggered back, plucking it out with his fingers.

Kane, ready for the slightest opportunity, was already in motion. Without questioning his reprieve, he dropped straight down, scooped up his revolver, and began shooting. Schlesinger was crying out a loud warning, his revolver aimed at the one stationary target—Dr Arling. Kane made a neat red hole in his shoulder, and the engineer dropped the weapon, lurching sideways.

The Jamaicans were firing as fast as they could draw a bead and pull the trigger, but the rifles were only single-shot, allowing Kane a grace period of a second or so to fire back selectively. One went down. A second looked at his compadre, threw away his gun and dashed for the woods. The last man dove behind some rocks, using them as a cover while he continued firing from their cleft. Kane felt a blow in his leg. He took a step, the leg giving out from under him, and he toppled off balance just while he was shooting at the negro. There was a peculiar chinking noise as the bullet missed its target and ricochetted off the rocks behind the man. The man screamed abruptly. Kane saw dark arms fly up from the rocks, the rifle clatter over the edge and hit the soft ground, and then the Jamaican rose up, clutching his cheek. He convulsed, vomiting blood, and fell across the rocks, the back of his skull missing and showing the pink mass of brains. The bullet had done its job anyway, veering to return and kill almost accidentally.

Not once did Colonel Valparaiso try to shoot Kane or Dr Arling. He'd dropped his rifle and was slowly wandering around in a daze, falling to his knees and shuddering in terror. He raised his hands beseechingly toward the lady doctor, who'd been standing rooted to the spot. "Madre Dios, Doctor," he whimpered. "I've been poisoned. Help me, I pray."

Gwen jumped to life, but Kane caught her arm before she could reach the stricken Colonel. "Let him die," he snarled. "He deserves it. Besides, you can't save him, nobody can."

"I can try," she snapped, and wrenched herself free.

The strength ebbed from Kane; he was unable to stop her. He saw her run to the Colonel and two slim silhouettes dart from the woods and run after her. He nodded, smiling ironically, recognising them as coastal Indians—two of her loyal natives. He wondered vaguely how far the Jamaican named Bobo got before he earned the swift sting from their blowpipes. Dully he tried opening the cylinder of his pistol and ejecting the spent cartridges, but now even the grip seemed too heavy for him. He stood tottering, while around him gathered yells and the noise of tramping feet.

The fever again, he thought dreamily. I've got the fever again. . . . It's because of the fever that I hear Lieutenant Sebaco and Mel Houston. . . . Fever. . . .

Then Kane blanked like a blown-out candle.

12

The port of Colon was teeming with boats in the amber sun of late afternoon. Morgan Kane sat on the balcony with his bandaged leg propped up on a stool, and wished he were someplace else. Lovely as it was, after two weeks of it, it bored him silly.

He reached for the jug of gin and lemonade beside him on a wicker table, ignoring the huge basket of fruit the Panamanian Governor had sent. Even for a governor, he wouldn't touch the stuff. Gin helped the most; after a few snorts, he didn't mind looking down at his pale, almost waxy skin, and flesh which had lost ten pounds from malaria.

The room of his suite opened behind him. He didn't bother turning around, knowing it was Doctor Arling for her routine daily visit. She came out on the balcony, looking sunbronzed and healthy, full of efficiency and bright spirits. It made Kane sick just to look at her.

"Well, and how are we today?" she chirped.

"*We* are feeling like hell," Kane grumped. "Just like *we* have been for two weeks now. Get this fool bandage off me!"

"Patience, Mr Kane, you must have patience."

"You're doing this on purpose, you know that, don't you?"

"I'm doing nothing of the kind."

"I talked to the hotel Doc, and he said it could've been taken off days ago."

"Pouf! What does that blind sawbones know? Besides I like you better all wrapped up. You're less of a menace then!"

"Who, to you?"

"To everybody. Now lie still while I wash you." Gently she unbuttoned his pajamas and cleaned his healing wounds with something that smelled like carbolic acid. "A day or so more is all, I promise," she told him when finished. "There's no sign of infection."

"Hasn't been, either. Alright, what do I owe you?"

It was a malicious reference to the first time she'd cared for him, on board the boat. She smiled at his joke, tapping the jug. "Repay me with local medicine. Will you play host?"

Kane poured a glass full of the lemonade concoction, and handed it to her from the tray. "Here."

"Thank you." She sipped it, settling herself in the chair across from Kane and smiling vaguely out at the dying sun. Kane frowned at her, for this had been the first time she'd made any gesture toward staying, much less having a drink with him. It made him nervous, and he sought something to say to her.

"I . . . ah, that is, when are you going back, Gwen?"

"Oh, not for some time. When I do, I think I might go out west. Our people need doctors, too, and I understand it's just as rough as anything down there."

"In its own way, I suppose it is."

"And you?"

"Like a flash, just as soon as I'm able to. I—" He was interrupted by a knocking on the door, and then Irving Randolph burst into the room, his hound-dog face lined with smiles. "Hello, Morgan—ah, and Gwen, m'dear. Quick, give me a drink too, it must've been a hundred and fifty in the courtroom."

Kane grumbled something under his breath about intrusions at the wrong time, but poured the reporter a glass. Gwen waited till Randolph was seated on the settee next to the table, before asking: "Well, what happened?"

"About as expected. Colonel Valparaiso was sentenced to a posthumous execution by firing squad, so it's just as well he died in the jungle. A nice touch of Latin justice, though, don't you think? Schlesinger will be going back to Nicaragua to stand trial there, but at least this way all the strings are wrapped up in a tidy bundle. It was him, all right. Behind the whole mess from the first, although when Kanter and his bodyguard muscled in on it later, he was more or less ousted from leadership."

"Did he go to them?" Kane asked, remembering his suspicion.

"No, he tried peddling some of the artifacts from the ruins, and Kanter got wind of it, since he was doing most of the illegal smuggling out of Colon through a phony import-export dealer. That's how the Hotchkiss rifles were brought in, by the way—Kanter's notion to help point blame at the French canal company if there was any trouble. Kanter wanted to make the operation really big, and get all the money out of the fort he could, and that was okay by Schlesinger. So Schlesinger talked Houston into setting up a supposed 'advance' camp, and Kanter supplied the Jamaican workers Schlesinger hired."

Kane swallowed his drink and poured another. "The heat evaporates this stuff," he said straight-faced, then: "Go on."

"Naturally the canal would eventually reach Schlesinger's site," Randolph continued. "So that's when the sabotage started, to postpone the work sufficiently to get all the treasure out. Colonel Valparaiso was brought in to help misdirect attention and keep the shipments moving smoothly, but Morgan, it was Schlesinger himself who manoeuvred you into the jungle, his Jamaicans did the sniping and then keeping you prisoner."

"But why?" Gwen asked. "Morgan wasn't after him."

"Not then, not yet—but Schlesinger was afraid Morgan might tumble to the setup. Morgan was the joker in the deck, you see, and had to be gotten rid of. So Schlesinger took it on himself to do it, and then he sent word to Kanter and Streicher to find out what they wanted done. Of course, Kanter was as surprised as anyone was. He and Streicher rushed up immediately, afraid that Schlesinger had panicked—which he had—and then they were doubly shocked when they learned from you that Morgan had escaped and was after their old demon."

"The monster alligator was a good stunt," Kane admitted ruefully. "It scared the natives away from the dig, and I've got to admit, it scared five years off my life too."

"It almost *took* your life, Morgan," Gwen noted pointedly. "But Irving, how did the Colonel get up there? And why?"

"Well, Kanter didn't tell Valparaiso why they were suddenly leaving Colon, and Valparaiso assumed it was because the ruins were finished and they were clearing out, double-crossing him. So he ordered the fastest boat he could and went straight to Schlesinger's camp, to get what was coming to him."

Kane added laconically: "He did."

"Last but not least, our brave Lieutenant Sebaco." Randolph raised his glass in a mock toast to the Nicaraguan soldier. "He'd been ordered to find you, Morgan, or your body, and not come back till he had. Houston was offering a triple bonus to the man who succeeded, so Sebaco had to go out there searching with his crew. They were close by the camp when the shooting broke out, and stormed in after it was all over."

"All over," Kane sighed, closing his eyes wearily.

"Not quite," Randolph said. "Not till we get you smuggled out of this hotel. There's a mob waiting by the entrance for when you finally make your appearance. You're a hero, Morgan, and the Nicaraguan Ambassador has a lovely platter of a medal for you—a decoration for 'The Heroic Achievement for the Nicaraguan Republic.' How's that for mud in your eye, eh?"

Kane shuddered in his chair as if he'd seen the old demon again.

"And naturally I've had to come up with a story on it," Randolph went on blandly. "Nothing much, you understand, Morgan. I mean, I understand and appreciate your desire to remain unnoticed."

"What have you written?" Kane asked warily.

"To show you my heart's in the right place, I'll even let you browse through my few notes." Randolph handed across a twelve-page story. Kane read the first line, then carefully ripped the report into tiny ribbons. He cast the shreds over the balcony, and watching them float away, Randolph added mournfully:

"Well, I tried."

"Anything else, Irving?"

He turned to Gwen, catching a strange gleam in her eye. "No, nothing. And I do believe that if I did, I'd better let it go for right now and leave."

"Oh, you don't have to so soon."

"Oh, yes I do, Gwen. I know that glimmer when I see it."

The doctor blushed. "Irving, don't you have your quinine to take about now? You wouldn't want to forget and become sick."

"Depends on the nurse I get." Randolph stood, polishing off his drink and smiling sardonically. "Like yours, Morgan . . . ?"

"*Tomorrow*, Irving!" Gwen snapped over the chuckles of the reporter as he sauntered from the room. The door shut, leaving Gwen and Morgan

Kane to look at one another in stiff embarrassment. "Well," she said, and glanced at her hands.

Kane cleared his throat. "Yes. Well."

Gwen smiled softly to herself, her face averted. She was embarrassed, but not in the way Kane imagined she was. She was ashamed of her shipboard appraisal of him, and the way she'd attacked him for being hardly more than a primitive savage. Gwen Arling was one of the few who'd seen Kane crumble to pieces—not much, but sufficiently to know there was a lonely man buried beneath his hard exterior shell. She realised now that life for Kane was an everlasting fight with men such as Kanter, Streicher, and others of their ilk, as demoniacal and as camouflaged as any dressed-up alligator hide could hope to be. It wasn't peculiar that Kane had become hard, brutal and suspicious from it all. She had felt his troubled doubt when he was sick and weak, and she had resisted its appeal. She had also felt his virile power, his strong magnetic attraction, and now she fought against that, too.

It was a fight she was losing. It was a fight that subconsciously, she knew she wanted to lose.

Kane asked distantly: "Since you won't saw the bandages off, Gwen, won't you stay for dinner here in my suite?"

"I would be pleased," she answered primly, and knew she sounded much more starched and proper than she felt. So she smiled to display her thanks and tone down the civility of her words. He smiled in response, the cold grey eyes becoming warm and vaguely soft. The mask over his emotions slipped, and the surprise of seeing him open to her made her laugh uncertainly. She placed a hand on his shoulder, as if she were trying to keep that smile and that freedom, and to stop the old Morgan Kane mask from sliding back in place. She liked the new Morgan Kane much, much more.

Kane gazed at this woman, and knew he would possess her that night. And he had the strange sensation of knowing how she would feel, pressed tightly to his naked body. He wondered about that, because his presentiments were always about life and death—and Dr Gwen Arling was neither of them.

He put his hand over hers, slowly and gently, and recalled his own comparison between her and Kate Coleman. Then he pushed the thought from his mind. He didn't like to be reminded about Kate, not when there was Gwen to think about instead.

EPILOGUE

Morgan Kane's brush with death, and the resultant malaria that was to plague him for the rest of his life, was for nought.

The French canal company under de Lessup's control went bankrupt two years later due to the physical problems of engineering and the disastrous wastage of funds through corruption. The French government guaranteed a loan of 720 million francs in 1888, but it was too little too late, and in March of 1889, the corporation was officially dissolved, and after a series of investigations, the courts prosecuted several prominent politicians and officials.

The Nicaraguan canal project continued until 1893, when the American company also went bankrupt. In the long run, the concept proved too expensive, although corruption was nowhere near as prevalent as in the French case. After the Spanish-American War, however, renewed interest in a canal stirred America into buying the Panamanian rights for forty million dollars. In 1903, America obtained a licence to a nine-mile-wide band across the recently established Panama republic, now independent of Colombia, and this cost an additional ten million dollars plus a yearly tax of a quarter of a million dollars. A series of locks were designed to cope with the different levels of the seas, and with thirty-five thousand labourers and new drugs against malaria and yellow fever, work was begun.

The Panama Canal was opened in 1914, just in time for World War I.

But by then, nobody knew where Morgan Kane was, or even if he were still alive. Whatever his reaction was to the news of the canal's opening was kept strictly to himself. . . .

THE END

SOUTHERN SHOWDOWN by LOUIS MASTERSON

For reasons he was doing his best to forget, Kane had turned in his marshal's badge back in Kansas City and drifted out east to Pasadena. He'd scraped together a few bucks hunting meat for the local cafe. But when Clive Van Doren hit town, Kane was hired to do a very different kind of hunting. Because as Van Doren's hired gun Kane's job was to kill one of the most notorious gunslingers in the West. But Kane soon found that, even without his badge, he was still a U.S. marshal and killing a man – any man – in cold blood just wasn't gonna' come too easy. . . .

0 552 10106 0 – 45p

I, TOM HORN by WILL HENRY

. . . I must leave this truth where it will be found. The story is all told, all written down, waiting only to be passed to the one who will get it from me tonight when he comes for the last time. No one could have told this story but me. I rode that trail in Wyoming alone. From the first day, it was Tom Horn against the pack. . . .

The Old West that Tom Horn knew lived and died with him. When he was gone the West was gone. In I, TOM HORN, Will Henry recreates the man and his times through a first-person narrative, as a possible lost autobiography of the legendary cowboy. Those who read it will always wonder . . . was this man guilty, or did his enemies kill him to make innocents of themselves?

0 552 10105 2 – 65p